WA
TH

BY

JAYNE BAULING

MILLS & BOON LIMITED
15–16 BROOK'S MEWS
LONDON W1A 1DR

First published 1982
Australian copyright 1982
Philippine copyright 1982
This edition 1982

ISBN 0 263 73781 0

Set in Monophoto Plantin 10 on 11 pt.

Made and printed in Great Britain by
Richard Clay (The Chaucer Press) Ltd,
Bungay, Suffolk

CHAPTER ONE

LESLEY would have denied that she was psychic, but occasionally a fey mood fell upon her, enabling her to perceive certain truths about people and events. No diviner of omens or reader of signs, she merely experienced feelings which were too potent to be ignored.

Now, fluttering her eyelashes at the face in the mirror, she was weighted by the sense that tonight's party was going to prove momentous. Knowledge of destiny, disastrous and shattering, swirled about her like an oppressive mist. This large, beautiful and soulless house was threatened, and she with it, and the danger was coming closer as if borne by the approaching storm which the thundery atmosphere heralded.

Like the men who shaved carefully and gave meticulous attention to dressing before going out to die, Lesley continued the application of her make-up, stroke by practised stroke, painting on the only face society was permitted to see. Ivory-tinted foundation and a dusting of a new cosmetic which gave her skin a pearlised gleam, soft green and silver about eyes with a slight, exotic slant, followed by kohl and a lavish application of mascara, roses blended into high cheekbones, and a bright red for her curving lips. Only her dark, beautifully shaped eyebrows were left untouched. This was her party face, but not so different from the one she presented every morning at lectures.

Glamour, glitter and sophistication; all belonged to Lesley, and no one seeing her could have suspected the mysterious currents of portent which governed her mind at this moment. Taking her time, she practised one of her smiles before leaving the dressing-table to slip into black silk stockings and a soft georgette dress of a black so rich as to make other blacks seem grey. It was slit at the left thigh, and its halter-neck left most of her smooth back bare, while it plunged sharply in front.

To complete the image she was intent on creating, she added strappy black sandals with thin, excessively high heels, the white sapphire ring and earrings which many people mistook for diamonds, and an extravagant dash of Joy. The bandeau came off her head next and her shining, dark brown hair was swept back from her face at one side and fastened with a glittery clasp but left falling in a small cascade of curls at the other side. She inspected herself in the full-length mirror, practised another smile and decided that her neck and cleavage looked naked without any adornment. Searching through drawers and boxes crammed with every imaginable item that the feminine heart might crave, she finally found what she was looking for, a narrow black band which she fastened about her neck so that its single red chiffon flower nestled against the fine skin just left of the hollow at the base of her smooth throat. She checked, found that it matched her lips and nails perfectly, and stepped back, well satisfied.

Still within her lay the recognition of *karma* in action, several factors converging to bring about one inevitable end, but Lesley was fey in another sense too, confident that she could turn back the incoming tide of disaster with one of her smiles. Hadn't she practised them all? And hadn't she always, since the age of sixteen, been in full control of every facet of her life? The physical storm might break, but the other one, gathering in her mind and stirring in her bloodstream, must surely be averted.

She left her bedroom and moved through the quiet

house with slow, deliberate grace, eyes resting on the familiar dark furnishings with little pleasure, although every item was antique and carefully chosen by her mother. The house was silent, none of their guests having yet arrived, and she decided reluctantly that now was as propitious a time as any to greet her parents and allow her father to initiate the usual perfunctory question-and-answer session which he felt the end of each university term warranted.

She had come home for the long summer vacation that afternoon, but her father had been out at his offices and her mother closeted with her beautician and hairdresser. Valerie Crosnier's position in society meant that she could summon such people to her instead of going to them. So too could her daughter, had she so wished, but Lesley preferred to trust her own hands in an art she had developed to a high level of proficiency.

She found her parents in her father's study, sipping sherry and talking desultorily, and she stood watching them for a while, impressed as always by her mother's elegant beauty and her father's good looks.

Valerie, magnificent in olive green and heavy gold jewellery, raised her flawlessly coiffured head. 'Lesley Ann,' she murmured faintly before stirring herself to greater interest. 'You'll have to change, my dear. You look like a tart.'

Bitter-sweet smile, Lesley decided, and produced it with facile accuracy. 'That was my intention,' she declared with delicate amusement.

Gerard Crosnier had stony, inexpressive brown eyes, but his smile was white and flashing, that of a politician or an evangelist. His daughter, however, was rarely its recipient.

He said bluntly, 'The whole of Johannesburg is talking about you.'

Another smile, tolerantly amused this time. 'Hardly the whole of it, Daddy. It's a big city. Just our circle.'

'All right!' But he was working up to a rage now and his wife directed a reproachful look at Lesley. Gerard was all Valerie's world and anyone who upset him was the enemy, even their own daughter. 'Not only our social circle, however, but my business acquaintances too.'

Lesley sank gracefully into a luxuriously upholstered chair, stretching out one small elegant foot and examining it complacently before suggesting lightly, 'What harm can that do? I wouldn't have thought they had any more scruples than you.'

'Lesley Ann!' Her mother was positively venomous by this time.

'Your behaviour is deliberate, isn't it?' Gerard challenged in a choleric splutter. 'Aimed at making me a laughing stock.'

'Oh, no.' Lesley moved her head gently from side to side, her voice a cold little sliver of sound. 'You haven't been the reason for any of my actions apart from my decision to move into residence, and that, allow me to point out, has proved restrictive to my . . . er . . . activities. I would enjoy greater freedom of movement living at home.'

'And that's another thing,' her father accused. 'It's ridiculous, your being in residence when your home is in the same city as the university. I should never have agreed to pay the fees. People are saying that your mother and I have washed our hands of you.'

'And haven't you?' She widened her eyes, but they remained unreadable, the green of a lake in shadow. 'Why should the truth worry you?'

'We've our good name to think of,' her mother reminded her coldly.

'Your good name?' Lesley's eyebrows rose in mocking enquiry. 'I don't think it's such a good name. People talk about you as much as me, Daddy, and your reputation is not flattering. Unscrupulous is one of the words. You'll recall that it was my discovery that you were evicting those O.A.P.s that prompted me to move into residence. But please, do my ego a favour and tell me what else is being said about me.'

'I've no intention of repeating what's being whispered,' Gerard stated with a belated attempt at dignity.

'Not shouted?' Lesley made herself look disappointed.

'Yes, shouted!' He himself was shouting suddenly, but his wife's hand on his arm caused him to draw a calming breath before continuing more quietly. 'Anyway, you must have a damned good idea of the things that are being said. If the word unscrupulous is associated with me, the one they're applying to you is . . . nymphomaniac!'

'And who constitutes the influential they?' Lesley asked with barely a pause to assimilate the word.

'Suffice it to say that the talk begins with Neville and all the other young men you've been out with.'

'Oh, Neville and company.' She was icily scornful. 'Would you believe me if I told you that everything Neville says about me is a lie? He has his reasons, as do the others.'

'A lie or not, it remains that you have this reputation, whether based upon fact or fiction,' her mother inserted. 'Naturally your father and I dislike it.'

'For your own sakes or mine?'

'Enough of this!' Gerard thundered. 'I've more important things to think of, and our guests will start arriving soon.'

'You've just said it all, Daddy,' Lesley said with mocking sadness, and there was a pause.

'Will you have a glass of sherry?' Gerard asked eventually.

'I'll wait until the champagne bottles are opened, thank you.'

Another pause, then, 'Well, I suppose you'd better tell me how your end of year exams went?'

'Brilliantly, as the results should confirm.'

'I'm surprised you find time to study,' her mother commented spitefully.

'And now you've . . . what? Two months' vacation?' Gerard asked vaguely, clearly losing interest in her now.

'Just about.' Lesley stood up swiftly. 'I think I'll go and find Lizzy, if you'll excuse me now.'

'What do you intend doing?'

'During the vac? Oh,' she paused at the door, expression mischievously demure, 'painting the town red, something like that.'

Feeling that she had acquitted herself quite well, Lesley departed, not to find Lizzy, because the maid would be in one of her temperamental pre-party moods, but to wander out to the patio and from there into the extensive gardens which Absalom kept in such exquisite order. Absalom cost the earth, but he didn't need telling what to do and her parents thought him worth it.

The evening sky was purple, with great banks of ominous coppery clouds piled on the horizon, and in the garden nothing stirred. It was as if every leaf and blade of grass was crushed down by an invisible weight, and the flowers had a bruised, suffering look as they waited for the still-distant storm to come and rend them from their stems.

Lesley laid her fingers flat against one cheek and was pleased to find that her silky skin remained cool. Her father hadn't been cool back there in the study.

She paused under the vines which sheltered a brick-paved walkway, wondering just how much she actually embarrassed her parents. She had spoken the truth in stating that her actions had nothing to do with them, but it was justice of a sort if they were embarrassed. After what they had done to Granny five years ago. Granny had been an embarrassment to them then; now she carried on the tradition.

Lesley stood removed from present reality, experiencing again the time when her paternal grandmother had lived with them. She had been a simple woman, proud of her son's success and wealth, devoted to her beautiful daughter-in-law, and her fifteen-year-old granddaughter's best friend. But she had worn the wrong clothes, talked too loudly and delighted in shocking Gerard's conservative acquaintances with her off-beat opinions. She was apt to sprinkle her conversation with curses in four languages, and on top of everything else, her beloved Irish terrier had sensed Gerard and Valerie's dislike and played up accordingly. Thus it was inevitable that Lesley should come home from school one day and find both grandmother and dog gone. It was the last time she had wept, both for what must surely be the old lady's sense of rejection and the animal's uncomprehending panic at being parted from the one human being he loved.

'It's for everyone's good,' Valerie Crosnier had said complacently.

'For your good, and Daddy's!' Lesley had screamed, fifteen years old and discovering disillusionment. It was also the last time she had lost her temper.

'We'll visit her at the home, of course.'

But the visits had grown few and far between, as other people more important than his mother had made calls on Gerard's time, until Lesley had had to resort to take a bus across town to spend the odd hour with the shockingly altered grandmother, holding her hand and inventing some fresh piece of wickedness Paddy might have perpetrated just the day before, lying as her parents had lied, but for a different reason, and learning too young about the things people did to each other, as cruel to their fellow human beings as they were to the birds and the beasts.

It had lasted but a short time. Within a year, the old lady had died—of a broken heart, Lesley was convinced.

Well, no matter now. It was no longer important. People were people, good, bad and mostly indifferent, and she at least had no heart to be broken by any of them.

No heart, nor even any warm blood to be stirred by a smiling glance or the touch of a hand; only a mind which saw people too clearly, saw the aura of selfishness which sat like a red-brown haze around her father's head, and saw the smallness of men like Neville who lied about her.

Men Lesley despised and was, at twenty, dedicated to making fools of as many as would fall down at her feet and worship the beautiful female form while caring nothing for Lesley Ann. She had been sixteen when first boys and soon men had started looking at her. She had begun the high school ritual of dating, expecting that soon one of the young men she went out with would prove to be the one who could create in her all those feelings described by the other girls at school: breathlessness, unbearable excitement, tenderness, accelerated pulse rate. But those sensations never came. True, she had warmed to some of the more patient young men, but it was then that she realised the curse of seeing into people. No one could delude her. Their motives came at her like a laser and, disappointed once again, she would turn away and look elsewhere.

For a while she had tried to discourage interest in her. In her last year at school she had altered her appearance drastically. Not quite as beautiful as her mother, she had been able to make herself look quite plain, but it hadn't worked. She couldn't change her increasingly beautiful body and she had learned painfully that not even her face was of interest to the opposite sex, let alone her mind.

Since then her tactics had altered and now she was so beautiful that men were awed by her even while they desired her, which suited her perfectly: they accepted her tactful 'no', believing that when so exciting a woman froze on them, the fault must lie with themselves.

Lesley listened to the sound of cars being halted on the other side of the house and smiled into the darkness. Neville would undoubtedly be at the party, and several others like him to whom she had at some time or another uttered that delicately regretful 'I'm sorry . . .' Civilised men who accepted it, but whose conceit was such that they must needs lie in their egomaniacal male conversations and add Lesley Ann Crosnier to the list of women they had won, each of them believing that every man she had been out with had succeeded where he himself had failed, and feeling unable to admit such defeat.

And hearing, as she always did, of their boasting, the slandered girl would produce her most maliciously amused smile and continue the game with whoever happened to be currently courting her surrender, and he too would fail and believe himself the only one.

'I'm frigid, I'm a virgin and nobody knows,' Lesley whispered the chant to the vine and turned to go and join the party which would end hours from now with a champagne breakfast. Not even her parents would believe the truth; not even Chrissie—the only friend of her own sex she had, for women dislike and fear others if they attract too many men.

'I thought I told you to change!' her mother hissed as Lesley brushed past her in the vast lounge which opened on to a veranda.

'Did you think I would?' Lesley retorted pleasantly, flashing her brightest social smile at Thelma, her godmother and her mother's best friend, and earning herself a look of disapproval from that most respectable of women.

The younger guests had congregated on the veranda, Neville and several other ex-boy-friends among them, mostly young executives and the like whose parents were known to hers, for theirs was a closed circle, exclusive and occasionally suffocating. Soon Lesley was surrounded, mysteriously slanting eyes sparkling as she worked her magic, her lovely mouth drawing on its range of a thousand smiles, never two the same and every one practised in front of a mirror.

Her mother was the most beautiful woman present tonight, with her dark skin and hair, and eyes greener than her daughter's, but of the younger generation only Petra could compete with Lesley and when they caught each other's eye, they smiled bright smiles, each faintly despising the other, seeing too clearly what she was.

Lesley knew a sudden sense of *déjà vu*. This was a party she had attended before, sometimes here, sometimes at someone else's home. The faces were the same. She had been out with every young man on this veranda. No, there was one she hadn't encouraged, eighteen-year-old Kim Lenny, but he must have finished school by now, so she would talk to him. He was very young, but captivating him would be less of a strain than enchanting some of these more sophisticated men, although all of them were under thirty.

Lesley smiled derisively into Neville's still bemused but traitorous eyes and drifted away to where the boy was standing alone, obviously ill at ease and too shy to approach anyone.

'Exams all over?' Her smile was bewitching, her shade-green eyes said he alone interested her, and her low voice was exquisitely musical and delightfully accentless.

'Praise be,' he confirmed fervently.

'What will you do?'

'Follow in my father's footsteps.' He laughed self-consciously.

Another one, Lesley thought resignedly, but she set herself out to charm, and soon he was growing loquacious under her flattering interest. Not yet set into a man's figure, he was thus looselimbed and clumsy; he was too eager, he tried too hard, but even he could not arouse compunction in the girl, because one day he would be like all the others.

She had forgotten her earlier presage of something momentous destined to occur tonight, but now it returned to her, as if the danger was drawing inexorably closer. Smiling at Kim, she was listening to the conversation about them, trying to identify what it was that was out of kilter, oppressing her with its threat of disaster, but the pattern of the party seemed to be the usual one.

'Gerard and Valerie do these things so well.'

'Don't they?'

'They employ a wonderful staff, of course.'

'They can afford to.' Envy there.

'Look at Lesley Ann.'

'Incredible!'

'Neville says she ...' The salacious voice was lowered.

'Who's the boy?'

'Who's the cradle-snatching vamp in black?'

This last arrested Lesley's attention. Derisive as the words were, the low male voice was attractive with its underlying note of amusement. Slowly, wondering, she removed her eyes from Kim's earnest young face and sought the speaker.

He stood at the open doors through which the high-pitched throng in the lounge was visible, and Lesley fluttered her lashes outrageously to give herself recovery time, for she had received a small shock.

He didn't look like an intimate of her parents', nor did he look like a business acquaintance. He was dressed more casually than the other men present for a start, tieless and wearing simple close-fitting jeans and a plain shirt, but she barely gave his clothes a glance.

He was watching her, and for once in her life Lesley was disconcerted, because he did so with neither the admiration nor the opposing disapproval to which she was accustomed. Yet there was something which hinted at condemnation. The sensuous mouth was unsmiling and the eyes—but she couldn't see the eyes. They were shadowy and she couldn't even guess at their colour.

Lesley was very still, trying to see him as she saw other people, perceiving their truths, but a haze seemed to separate her from him and she felt chilled. It could be dangerous, to fail to understand a man who looked like this one. Tall and hard and strong and tanned, with dark brown hair dipping over his brow, he had the face, not of a cynic, but certainly of one who has seen it all and then some. It was an arresting face, with hollows beneath the high cheekbones and an aquiline nose, and as she stared at him he moved his lips in soundless question.

Lesley replied with her iciest, through-and-through stare, the one she usually reserved for the importunate and the persistent, and saw him smile. She transferred her attention to his companion and recognised Heather Louw, a rare guest at these social gatherings although she was always invited. She was someone apart, different from the other women in their circle yet, at twenty-six, as successful as any of them, the owner of a boutique which sold ravishing and exclusive garments of her own design, and Lesley was unsurprised that her partner should be as much someone apart as she was.

'Excuse me, Kim,' she begged charmingly. 'There'll be dancing later and I'll see you then, but I must say hullo to Heather.'

With deliberately graceful movements she made her way towards the couple at the doors, keeping her eyes on Heather's dusky gamine face but fully aware that the man watched her approach.

'Heather!' she greeted her, admiring the soft brown hair which was beautifully layered to reveal the perfect shape of her head and tiny ears, and briefly wishing she could achieve that tasteful, ladylike look. 'We don't see you at these flings too often. How are you?'

Heather's velvety brown eyes were friendly. 'I'm afraid I'm into early nights with a book or television, Lesley. You wouldn't have seen me here tonight either, had I not told Rad here about my invitation. For some reason he decided I should accept it and let him accompany me, so . . . here we are! This is Rad Sinclair. Rad—Lesley Ann Crosnier.'

He shook his head mockingly. 'Lesley Ann is a little girl's name.'

'Just plain Lesley suits me better,' she assured him with a melting smile and one of her devastating oblique glances.

He was unaffected but said gallantly, 'Anything but plain. That dress was never a product of Heather's genius.'

'Regretfully, no.'

'Lesley has a very individual style for which I couldn't possibly cater,' Heather explained, smiling.

Rad Sinclair laughed. 'What a kind young woman you are, Heather.'

His eyes came to rest on Lesley once more and she saw that they were a dark, smoky grey.

She said lightly, 'Pictures of you always show a beard, Rad Sinclair.'

'Necessity, not choice. I was glad to get home and remove it.'

'I know all about you, of course,' she continued.

'Now, that I doubt,' he countered sceptically.

With justification, she realised. Even now she wasn't seeing him clearly.

'The facts,' she qualified. 'Rad Sinclair, correspondent for one of our leading newspapers. You've been everywhere and seen everything. You were wounded by gunfire while covering a war on the bulge of Africa and have come home on leave to recuperate. Let me add, although I'm sure you don't need it, that I actually read what you write. I thought your study of the Khmer Rouge was particularly good.'

'Wild disbelief. You actually read?'

'Education remains compulsory,' she reminded him demurely.

'But newspapers?' He was still pretending scepticism. 'What else do you do, Lesley Ann Crosnier?'

'If anything?'

'If anything.'

'I've just completed my second year at Varsity.'

'Degree? Don't pile on any more shocks!'

'I won't. B.A.'

'You relieve me.' He smiled tauntingly. 'Blow All.'

'Please!' Lesley protested vivaciously with an elegant

gesture of one hand. 'Don't tone it down for my sake. I have heard the alternative word, despite my tender years, and I also have a knowledge of journalists.'

'An extensive one, I have no doubt, knowing my own breed pretty well.' He paused. 'But the milder word was for Heather's sake, not yours.'

Lesley widened her eyes innocently. 'Now why should Heather merit such consideration, but not me?'

'Heather is a lady.'

'Honestly, Rad!' Heather gave him a little push, looking pleased but embarrassed. 'Ignore him, Lesley.'

'But I agree with him, Heather. You're nice and you're a lady—the only one here tonight.'

'Better and better,' Rad approved sardonically. 'Not only does she possess reading ability, but she's perspicacious as well.'

'Very, I should think,' Heather agreed lightly. 'So, I'll tell you what, Rad. You wanted verbal pictures of several of the people around us and I'm so out of touch that I couldn't provide them, so why not let Lesley try while I go and talk clothes with a rival I've just spotted?'

'Ah, but can you do so without bias?' he enquired as Heather moved away from them. 'No, don't stir, Lesley Ann. We're at a good vantage point here, with both those inside and those on the veranda visible.'

Lesley had to tilt her head in order to look into his face. She was a mere five-foot-five, and even her very high heels didn't raise her to his height, since he must be all of six foot.

Her smile was challenging. 'I'm just wondering why you of all people should be interested in anyone here. Can it be that you're turning your hand to writing a gossip column while you're absent from foreign wars? "The Lid Off The Northern Suburbs". Is that it?'

The grey eyes were shadowy and suddenly remote. 'Can't we just put it down to curiosity? I've been away from Jo'burg a long time.'

'The journalist's enquiring mind?'

'If you like. Here!' He had stopped a passing waiter hired for the occasion and was examining his tray. 'You're a champagne drinker or I'm a teetotaller.'

'I'd love to surprise you, but yes, I only drink champagne,' she conceded, red lips pouting reproachfully.

'Expensive,' he murmured, handing her a glass.

'But so nice. Who shall we start with?'

'What about that boy you deserted? Forlorn doesn't begin to describe him now,' he added amusedly.

'Oh, that's Kim Lenny. He wouldn't interest you,' Lesley assured him dismissively.

'Apparently he interested you,' Rad retorted drily.

'Possibly.' She made her smile mysterious.

'Or is it simply that he's the only male present whom you haven't so far had twined round your little finger?' he continued insultingly.

'Don't you mean twined round my body?'

'I think I meant both.' His eyes dropped from her face to her slim sexy body and he smiled. 'It's the body beautiful, anyway.'

'And its reputation is extensive.' This was a new game, but if she played it carefully she could enjoy it. She might even win it.

'What about the young man over there?'

'Neville?' Lesley grew gently sarcastic. 'Neville is perfect. He came out of a machine with a label and a guarantee: nothing can go wrong with this piece of equipment. He's the original up-and-coming-executive-about-town. He wears the right clothes and drives the right car. Nothing is too dull or too flashy. He says the right things to the right people and he tramples all over the wrong ones.'

'That's fairly comprehensive, but you've omitted one thing,' Rad suggested. 'He's one of Lesley Ann Crosnier's ex-lovers.'

'Where did you hear that?' she asked, carefully expressionless.

'I've been in Johannesburg long enough to encounter that particular rising young executive,' he informed her equivocally.

'Do all men kiss and tell?' she asked drily.

'All young men.'

'How old are you?'

'Too old for you.' His smile was a taunt. 'Thirty-six.'

'Married?'

'No.'

'Why not?'

'That's a question that has no simple answer. Perhaps it has no answer of any sort but, remember, I'm rarely in one place for long.'

'And what woman wants a husband who goes chasing after danger?' she suggested.

'Try to sound concerned!' he grinned.

'Why? I'm sure you take your pleasure where you find it,' she countered sweetly.

'How wise you are, Lesley,' he mocked.

'Too wise.'

'Is that a warning?'

'Perhaps it's a threat.'

'You're not my type, darling,' he said smoothly.

'Just as well, since I don't like you, Sinclair,' Lesley answered with a wide and beautiful smile. 'Darling. Perhaps Petra is your type?'

'The genuine platinum blonde with the violet eyes and Bo Derek's figure?'

'And all of it on show. That one isn't a lady either.

The tart with heart.'

'And a better woman than you, my dear,' he said, scorn suddenly showing through the air of reserve he had never completely discarded.

'Why?'

'When she smiles, she doesn't think about it first.'

'A bad mistake.'

'In your book. Personally I prefer women who are human enough to make the occasional mistake.'

'There should be plenty to your liking, then, since most of my sex seem to spend their lives landing in hot water. It's not for me, though.' Strangely she was feeling suddenly vulnerable, gripped by a need to defend herself.

'We must pursue this some other time, I think.' Rad said coolly. 'Who are the couple holding the floor inside?'

'William and Thelma, my godparents.'

'Tell me about them.'

'You have to be planning an exposé of northern suburbs society,' Lesley laughed. 'You'll find nothing improper about William and Thelma, however. They're very proper people. In fact there are so many subjects Thelma regards as unmentionable that one scarcely dares utter in her presence. Not that she expects you to. She holds court.'

'What does William do?' Rad put the question idly, but his glance had sharpened. 'Is he associated with any of your father's various concerns?'

'No.'

'I know which is your father, of course, but which is your mother?'

'The beautiful one.'

'I think I should introduce myself to them.'

'My father doesn't like the press,' Lesley warned him calmly. 'They once had him featuring as villain of the week when he evicted some old age pensioners from flats in several blocks he owns.'

'I doubt if that's the only crime he has ever committed,' Rad said expressionlessly. 'I think I'll risk meeting him. We'll meet again later, Lesley.'

They would too, she was sure. The night was not yet very old.

CHAPTER TWO

THE storm was closer now. Thunder rumbled ominously and flickers of lightning lit the summer sky, but the dancers on the veranda kept up their rhythmic actions. Lesley danced as beautifully as she walked, just sexily enough to be enticing without being blatant, and still a series of wonderful smiles illuminated her face.

Her mind was shrieking, however. Kim Lenny was boring, boring, and the December night was too hot. It threatened, and a sense of doom threatened until she felt crushed by their joint weight, unable to rid herself of the conviction that whatever disaster was imminent, Rad Sinclair was to be its catalyst.

She had seen him stroll over and introduce himself to her father; seen too Gerard's momentarily ill-concealed displeasure before the wide, white public man's smile had flashed out. Later she had watched the pair of them disappearing in the direction of Gerard's study, and had wondered.

They had not reappeared and she continued to speculate. It was something to think about while she pretended to be listening to Kim.

'You don't mind if I claim this next dance?' Suddenly he was there, addressing the boy as they stood between dances, waiting for the music to be resumed.

Kim looked resentful, but there was little protest he could make in the face of the older man's easy self-confidence and he stepped aside with a polite nod.

'You didn't ask if I minded,' Lesley pointed out with

a provocative pout as the music started up again.

'Do you?'

'Not really, but it would have been nice if you'd asked. Politeness, you know.'

'Token politeness.' Rad was scathing. 'I'm not a member of your circle, Lesley, so don't expect me to display the superficial good manners you people seem to find so important, if only because they cover the internal rottenness.'

The sentiment surprised her slightly, since it was one she had shared at times, and she was silent for a few moments. The number playing now was a slow one and usually she hated the physical contact required by this sort of dancing, but Rad held her lightly yet firmly and not too close. Nevertheless, she was rigid with the tension which was habitual to her when anyone touched her, but he made no comment, so perhaps he hadn't noticed.

'You're in a bad mood,' she ventured challengingly.

'Clever girl,' he drawled.

'I suppose you tried to interview my father?'

'Let's put it this way: I asked him a few questions.' His smile was grim.

'And the answers weren't satisfactory.'

'On the contrary, they were all too satisfactory.' The smile had disappeared and he looked down at her impatiently. 'Why don't you shut up for a while and concentrate on dancing?'

Obediently Lesley did so, but light conversation, as much as smiling, was a part of her armour against being revealed to callous eyes and she found it difficult. She was still unable to sense the essential truth of this man as she was able to do with other people and she was in danger of panicking. Somehow she couldn't see him clearly. She didn't even know whether he liked or despised her, and such uncertainty made her feel vulnerable.

She looked up into his face. He seemed just barely aware of her and the fact that they were dancing together, as if other things altogether occupied his mind. His shadowy grey eyes were remote and so dark that they looked almost black.

For the first time Lesley noted the look of tiredness about them and tried to recall all she knew about Rad Sinclair, which was little enough, since few pressmen achieved or even wanted the fame of Woodward and Bernstein. They kept themselves private and exposed others to the world's prurient gaze.

He was a man who had seen hell, she thought, recalling some of the places and situations he had written about. He must despise people like her and her friends who went about their comfortable lives with the vaguest knowledge of the anguish existent in various parts of the world, yet only occasionally had he allowed his contempt to show tonight. Otherwise he was relaxed and confident, too together to be cynical. Reading his reports, Lesley had sensed a passionate caring; it had never been emotional, but always rational, leading her to respect the writer.

Now she wanted to know more, fascinated even while she disliked him and feared his unknowability. A man who had travelled too far and seen too much, looked under stones for the darkness of human nature and seen atrocities committed in bright sunlight. He had probably indulged in excesses but, too, his sojourns in the strange, fearful countries governed by madmen would have demanded tremendous self-discipline and the need to be alert at every moment.

He would work and he would relax, taking what pleasure offered itself. Was it pleasure that had brought him here tonight?

She said carefully, 'You look tired. Was your injury bad?'

The strong masculine features took on a guarded expression. 'Not in itself. A simple shoulder wound, but for a while after it happened it was only receiving the minimum of treatment.'

'I'm beginning to remember,' Lesley said slowly. 'You were imprisoned, weren't you?'

'Yes.' He sounded bored. 'In the prevailing chaos up there, someone in what authority still existed decided that I must be a South African spy. Fortunately I hold a British passport since I was born in Scotland, and the Embassy was able to get me released when things had calmed down a bit.'

'What was it like?'

Rad gave an exclamation of disgust and Lesley felt the impatient tension that suddenly filled him.

'Even if you were a man, I wouldn't tell you.'

'It was a silly question.' She smiled her apology quite ravishingly. 'But why do you do it, Sinclair?'

'Why not? Someone has to, and I've no parents or wife to make me feel guilty about exposing myself to danger, besides which, in most countries the press, foreign or local, enjoys a measure of immunity.'

'But you've been offered editorships on a number of occasions, haven't you?'

'You're very well informed.' His smile was sardonic.

Normally Lesley was resigned to men viewing her as an entirely physical entity devoid of intellect, and was secretly amused by their mistake, but now a wave of irritation washed over her.

'Why does that fact require comment? I'm not stupid, Sinclair.'

'You're not, are you?' he concurred, mildly amused. 'In fact, I'm sure you're highly intelligent . . . probably too intelligent for your own good. It's just a pity that you didn't aim higher than a B.A. What are you majoring in, incidentally?'

'English and history.' She looked up at him through long dark lashes. 'I suppose you feel I should be doing something . . . useful to society? I could become one of those socialites who do voluntary nursing and raise funds for charities. My mother does the latter.'

Rad laughed. 'I can't see you in that rôle, darling. No, I meant—why didn't you consider something more intellectually challenging?'

'What for?' Lesley shrugged gracefully. 'I doubt if my brain is ever going to play a major part in determining the events of my life.'

'In other words, your face is your fortune?'

'Not just my face, Sinclair,' she retorted gently.

'Not just your face,' he seconded smoothly. 'Shall we go into the garden for a while?'

'I thought you'd never ask!' Lesley taunted provocatively.

'I didn't think you'd be backward in doing the asking yourself,' Rad countered as they left the lighted veranda and moved into the shadowy garden.

'Perhaps I'm old-fashioned,' she murmured facetiously.

His laughter was low-pitched and attractive. 'That I can't believe.'

Now that she was alone with him, without a protective press of people about them, Lesley felt strangely breathless. It was ridiculous, she assured herself, because they would merely enact a scene which she knew too well already and which she could handle with perfect ease. The trouble was that Rad Sinclair was older than any of the other men with whom she had played this game, more experienced and surer of himself. Safer, perhaps, to have stayed with Kim Lenny, but less exciting.

Exciting? Oh, but nothing and no one excited her. Rad would ultimately prove to be just like all the others who had been so greedily intent on their own pleasure that never one of them had felt her freezing, devouring her and failing to sense her withdrawal until she uttered the familiar words, 'No, I'm sorry . . .'

She led him to the vine-covered walk where earlier that evening she had whispered aloud the truth about herself. It must be close to midnight now and the storm would soon be overhead. Jagged streaks of lightning lit the sky, thunder cracked and roared, just a few miles away, and the heat of the night was something torrid and sultry, a pulsating pressure which could explode into fragments at any minute.

Lesley stopped and turned to face her companion. She felt oddly unsure of herself and when she spoke she knew she sounded hostile.

'This will do. Let's get it over with.'

A blaze of lightning revealed his bland countenance.

'Why do you imagine I asked you to come outside?' he questioned her in a silken tone.

Lesley produced an incredulous little laugh. 'Why, either to ask me to go out with you some time, which you could have done on the veranda, or to kiss me, of course. Men never suggest a walk in the garden with any other motive.'

'Your men.' Rad's voice had grown cold. 'I told you you weren't my type.'

Relief was a shocking, weakening thing, but with it came the return of her wit. 'I do believe you've surprised me, Sinclair,' she murmured faintly, deciding that a smile would be wasted in the darkness.

'I'll bet I have, my pretty young vamp,' he said brutally. 'I intend surprising you still more.'

'I can hardly wait!'

'The game stops here and now, Lesley,' he warned quietly.

'A pity. I was enjoying it.'

'God, but you're an exasperating young woman!' he flared with sudden impatience. 'I don't know why I'm bothering when I'm sure you're eminently capable of taking care of number one. Still, for what it's worth, I advise you to get out now.'

Lesley hesitated and decided on honesty. 'I'm not with you, Rad. Get out?'

'Yes, get out, pull out, make arrangements, put your house in order,' he elaborated disgustedly. 'The whole business is going to blow up under you very shortly and there'll be a lot of people crying for blood, as you can imagine.'

'No, I can't imagine,' Lesley replied sharply. 'I still don't know what you're talking about.'

'You're truly your father's daughter, aren't you?' he lashed with sudden contempt. 'He too played the innocent, denied any knowledge of what I was talking about, but the facts speak for themselves, I'm afraid. I thought your youth, however despoiled, merited a warning, but if you're determined to play ostrich . . .'

Lesley was silent for a few moments, hiding her bewilderment as best she could, before saying in a clear little voice, 'I get it, Sinclair. You're bored being on leave, away from the action, so you're concocting petty little intrigues with which to entertain yourself.'

'I'm not officially on leave until next week,' Rad told her expressionlessly. 'And believe me, Lesley, what's cooking is far from petty.'

'Surely the Wicked Landlord spiel is small beer for a man like yourself,' she continued icily. 'It's been done so many times before, and my father has even featured in the title rôle. Why not try investigating industrial espionage instead? That should be worthwhile.'

'God, you're really adept at deceiving yourself. All right, forget it, and I hope you enjoy the consequences.'

She probably would too, Lesley reflected drily. There was no affection between her and her parents, so she could enjoy the spectacle of their embarrassment, even knowing resignedly that Gerard Crosnier would always rise to the top again. You couldn't sink him permanently.

'Was that all?' she queried with chilling softness.

'Yes, since you persist in this wilful blindness,' Rad answered violently. 'But no, on second thoughts, I don't want to disappoint you too severely. Come here.'

Lesley was drawn roughly into his arms, imprisoned against the hard length of his body, and his lips were forcing hers apart. Shocked, she stood very still, not attempting to struggle. She had never been kissed so contemptuously, so angrily, before, and the experience was humiliating. Her body was pressed relentlessly to his, enabling her to realise that Rad was experiencing none of the masculine arousal she was accustomed to in the men who kissed her. Simply, he was very angry and totally disgusted, therefore he was punishing her.

It was a mortifying aeon of time before that shattering kiss ended, with never a single caress to soften its terrible impact, but when Rad did release her, he did so abruptly, virtually flinging her from him.

Lesley, however, still regarded herself as a match for any man, even this violent one who was a stranger to the coy niceties inherent in the other men she knew.

Voice an icy trickle of sound, frost-silver, she said, 'You'll forgive my lack of response, I'm sure, when I say I've never been kissed in anger before.'

'I'm damn sure you haven't,' he taunted. 'Even if any of your vacuous young men have ever experienced such a red-blooded emotion as anger, you won't have been the catalyst. No, Lesley Ann Crosnier is quite delightfully easy, always willing to please.'

'I'd rather please them than you.'

'Careful. You're sinking below your normal level now, darling, not that that's any too high.' He paused contemplatively. 'I wonder what they see in you? No, I don't. I know too well. Even in your parents' home, Neville wasn't averse to mentioning your performance in the bedroom.'

'You too are sinking below your normal level,' Lesley pointed out calmly. 'Insults are childish.'

'Is the truth ever an insult?' Rad countered. 'It is the truth, isn't it, Lesley Ann? You're nothing but a tart, and you deserve a tart's fate. You're not even a challenge, so I'll say goodnight now and collect Heather. I'm sure she's had a surfeit of the company here, just as I have.'

'You won't stay on? The storm won't last long and there is a champagne breakfast later,' Lesley said in her best hostess manner.

'No, thank you.' Rad was emphatic.

'Excellent.' Now her voice dripped honey and a lightning flash revealed a smile to match, although her lips had been denuded of their artificial colour by the harsh pressure of his. 'Goodbye, then, Rad, and I hope I never see you again.'

His laughter was sardonic. 'If you're wise, you won't. You play to the bitter end, don't you?'

'Who's bitter?' she asked nonchalantly.

'Nobody—yet. Goodbye, Lesley Ann.'

He strode away up the walk, disappearing into darkness, a man like no other she had met.

The stillness of the garden was disturbed by the first rough gusts of the wind which bore the coming storm, but Lesley remained where she was with the skirt of her dress whipping about her thighs. It was habitual for her to smile in triumph at the end of any encounter with a male and she did so now, but all that she actually felt was relief at Rad's departure.

She hadn't triumphed, and she knew it, but that hardly constituted the disaster of which her senses had earlier warned her. Rad Sinclair had come and gone and she would never see him again, and if his newspaper was contemplating an anti-Gerard Crosnier campaign, well, that had happened before and Gerard had sued a few people and the whole affair had died down fairly quickly.

Lesley stirred protestingly against the increasing violence of the wind and moved away towards a side entrance to the house, intent on repairing her make-up before rejoining the party which would have to move indoors from the veranda for perhaps an hour while the storm lasted.

When she sought out Kim Lenny again, Rad Sinclair and Heather Louw had gone, and she was glad. Rad was best forgotten quickly.

It was noon when Lesley awoke the next day. Apart from the servants the house appeared deserted, so her father was presumably at work and her mother still in bed. Outdoors, everything had a newly washed look as she headed for the swimming pool, but a few plants and shrubs had been laid flat by the storm and Absalom was muttering irately as he went about salvage operations.

Lesley swam, showered and dried her hair, changing its style and, once dressed and made up, she got out the car her father had bought her a year before and drove over to her friend Chrissie's home, not returning until evening.

Still there was no sign of her parents, and she sought out Lizzy in the kitchen while her bath was running.

'I won't be here for dinner, Lizzy. I'm going out,' she explained.

Lizzy shrugged plump shoulders, her black face the expressionless one of a good servant, tactful and discreet, although Lesley thought she probably despised them all.

'Then there's no one for me to cook for. Mr and Mrs Crosnier will be out as well.'

'Where?'

'Your mother didn't say, except not to wait up.' Lizzy returned to labelling spice jars and Lesley went to her bath.

Kim called for her in his father's car a little later and the relaxing afternoon she had spent ensured that Lesley was at her sparkling best. His ideas ran to nothing more exotic than a meal and a movie, but she didn't mind, and when he invited her to choose the film she mischievously selected a cartoon, since he was at the age to be embarrassed if anyone caught him at anything ostensibly childish.

Later when he took her home she suffered his clumsy embrace and several inconsiderate kisses before pushing him away and telling him to call her tomorrow.

She heard him drive away and retired to her room to set about her nightly beauty routine. She was bored, she realised, massaging cream into her slender legs. Another party was called for. Perhaps she could persuade Chrissie to throw one at her home, although if Chrissie's mother knew the idea came from Lesley she would refuse to grant her permission, since she disapproved of Lesley and regarded her as a bad influence on her daughter.

'My mother doesn't care who influences me,' Lesley had told Chrissie only that afternoon.

Her mother . . . Lesley got into bed. Tomorrow she must really make an effort to corner her mother and get her to ask Gerard for her allowance. She was down to her last few rand and there was Christmas coming up. She would buy herself some new clothes. Perhaps she could persuade her father to open a bank account for her . . .

The sound of the telephone woke her early in the morning, but it was quickly silenced and she turned over and drifted off to sleep once more. Then it sounded again—and again. By now other sounds were reaching her and she sat up irritably, glancing at the little gold clock beside her bed. It wasn't that early, but earlier than she was accustomed to getting up during vacation.

Lizzy, unusually, was shouting somewhere in the house and someone in the garden was shouting back at her, but it wasn't Absalom. In fact, it sounded as if there were a number of people in the garden.

Lesley lay back against the pillows. Probably the crowd in the garden were workmen. Her parents had long contemplated building on to the already large house, but there were going to be fireworks from Absalom if even one of his plants was damaged during the alterations.

At that moment her bedroom door was flung open and Lizzy appeared on the threshold.

'Miss Lesley, you get up now and speak to these people,' she begged, not at all her normal placid self.

Lesley sat up. 'What's going on?'

Lizzy was rapidly losing the command of English upon which Valerie insisted in her servants. 'Dese people outside and on de phone . . . I don't know what's happening.'

'Well, who are these people, for a start?' Lesley asked calmly as she got out of bed.

'Dey say from de newspapers, Miss Lesley.'

'Oh, my God!' Lesley hesitated. 'Well, can't my

father deal with them? He won't have left for work yet.'

'He's gone,' Lizzy wailed. 'Dey didn't come back last night, your father and mother. You come and speak to dese people, Miss Lesley.'

'I will . . . when I've showered and dressed,' Lesley promised, already at the bathroom door.

'You hurry!' Lizzy adjured.

'No, I won't hurry for them,' Lesley said coolly. 'I'll face them in full warpaint, Lizzy, and that takes time. Keep the doors locked and make me some coffee.'

Her mind was racing as she stood under the shower. That some story had broken, and it was Rad Sinclair's doing, she was convinced, but her parents' absence was inexplicable. She felt the first stirrings of fear. That sense of impending disaster she had experienced the other night and later attributed to the approaching storm making her over-sensitive . . . Had disaster come now?

She dressed in tight blue jeans and a floaty, transparent floral top. As Heather Louw had commented, her style was very individual and relied partly on the trick of teaming such casual garments as jeans with ultra-feminine tops. Back in her bedroom she made up her face as she sipped her coffee, while Lizzy agitated around her.

'Keep calm, Lizzy,' she said evenly.

'But what will happen?' Lizzy demanded.

'To you and me? Nothing at all, I'm sure. This concerns my parents.'

'But they've gone.'

'Where, I wonder?'

Finishing her face, the lovely mask which would protect her, Lesley parted her hair in the middle and clipped it back with two little pink heart-shaped clasps.

'We'll go out fighting, Lizzy,' she vowed, standing up. 'Come on. I'll go first. I hope they haven't damaged Absalom's plants.'

At the beautifully carved front door she paused. She needed to know what was happening before facing the press, but how was she to find out? Slowly she unlocked the door and drew it back, and almost gasped at the sight which met her eyes.

They were everywhere, with their recording machines and cameras, their cars parked in the street, the driveway, even on the lawn. Men and women, some sprawled on the lawn but springing up when she appeared, flashbulbs already exploding before she had a chance to fix the bright, meaningless smile on her face.

She caught sight of Rad Sinclair watching her enigmatically and her smile altered subtly as she beckoned to him, even while all the others surged forward.

'You'd better come in and tell me what's happening,' she whispered.

His fellow-journalists fell back as he indicated that he would enter the house alone and, once in, he shut and locked the door.

'Can Mr Sinclair have some coffee, please, Lizzy?' Lesley asked. 'We'll be in the lounge.'

'I admire your style,' Rad drawled as he followed her into the lounge.

'So do I,' Lesley laughed. 'Especially as I'm groping in the dark. You'd better tell me the worst.'

'The worst has happened,' he retorted. 'I did warn you, Lesley.'

'I'm beginning to wonder what you warned me of,' she said slowly.

'Isn't it time to stop this pretence of ignorance?' he snapped.

'It's no pretence, darling. I genuinely don't know what's going on, and my parents don't appear to be here.' She tried a smile.

A wary, taut look about the man arrested her. He was standing very still as he searched her face with shadowy grey eyes. Then he seemed to reach a decision.

'Just a moment.'

He left her and she heard him go outside again. Moments later he was back, carrying that morning's edition of his newspaper. 'Take a look at this.'

Lesley took the paper from him and flinched at the main headline which screamed her surname. The story below carried Rad's name.

'God!'

Her hands holding the paper were betraying her with a slight shake and even her make-up couldn't disguise the sudden draining of colour from her face which left her blusher standing out as two ridiculous smudges. She could hardly assimilate what she read because her eyes kept blurring and there was a dizzy emptiness which made her head feel light, but she was able to absorb the gist of the facts he had uncovered.

Gerard Crosnier's whole successful career had been based on a series of frauds and lies. The number of people he had cheated ran into hundreds. Half of it Lesley couldn't understand, but she understood the immorality of it, the cruelty to those who had put their faith in him. The very least of his sins, she gathered, had been the selling of flats not under sectional title, tax evasion and the illegal transfer of large sums of money to foreign banks. Charges were expected to be laid. There would be a sequestration order.

Lesley dropped the newspaper on to the thick carpet and walked across the room to stand below her mother's portrait, keeping her back to Rad.

'You didn't know.' He spoke flatly from behind her.

'You bastard,' Lesley whispered.

'Lesley——'

'For pity's sake!' she exclaimed shakily. 'If you speak to me I'll cry or curse, or both.'

'Perhaps you should.'

'Perhaps, but I won't. I won't cry, I never cry. Damn you, Rad Sinclair, why didn't you explain the other night?'

'I thought you knew.'

She turned round at that, dark green eyes dazzlingly bright. 'You thought I knew. Yes!' She smiled, but her lips quivered. 'All I knew was the landlord forever putting the rents up, evicting people who couldn't pay . . . I thought you were talking about that the other night. How could you think I knew? If I'd known all the rest, do you think I'd have been . . . associating with him, coming home for vacations? My God!'

'Lesley——'

'No!' she interrupted coldly. 'Don't explain. I know why you thought I knew, and I don't suppose I can blame you, but I still hate you, Rad Sinclair!'

'For what?' he challenged shortly.

'For . . . oh, I don't know. Forget it. I know you had to do it.' She was calmer now and she sat down as Lizzy entered the room with a tray bearing two cups and a jug of coffee. 'Thank you, Lizzy. I'll come and explain everything to you later. How do you like your coffee?'

'Black, please.' Rad sat down opposite her as Lizzy departed.

'You believe now that I knew nothing of my father's illegal activities?' Lesley enquired coolly as she poured the coffee.

'Yes.'

'Why?'

'You fake most things, my dear, but you weren't faking your reaction to that story,' he said mockingly as he took his coffee.

'I forgot to act,' she murmured flippantly, and saw him smile. 'Well! The fat's on fire, the cat is out of the bag, the dog has had his day and is about to be hauled over the coals . . . The question is, where are my parents? Lizzy says they didn't come home last night.'

Rad's eyes revealed nothing as he regarded her steadily. 'We received word while we were waiting outside that they flew out of South Africa late last night. I doubt if they'll return, Lesley.'

'That Swiss bank account?'

'Exactly.'

'So Daddy must have known it would all blow up one day and coldly prepared for that eventuality,' Lesley said. 'How . . . how terribly cynical!'

'You didn't even know that they were skipping? They said nothing to you?'

'I didn't see them yesterday.'

'They left no letter explaining things to you?' A note of anger had entered his voice.

'I don't know.'

'Go and look.'

But no note was to be found. Much had been left behind, for Gerard and Valerie had taken only their clothes and a few personal possessions. But those things they should have left behind—an explanation for their daughter and provision for her future, references for their servants—were absent, as Lesley shortly returned to tell Rad.

'You're going to have to get out of here,' he told her unemotionally. 'There'll be a sequestration order. Hundreds of people were cheated of huge sums by your father and they'll be demanding recompense. While you were searching the house I was on the phone to Ewart Brummer, your father's lawyer. He's a very disillusioned man, but he has agreed to handle as much of that side of things as he can, for your sake. He agrees that you'd be better off having nothing to do with it.'

'Yes. Well, that's that, isn't it?' Her voice was low and strained, but still she managed a smile. 'What about your colleagues outside? Do I have to speak to them?'

'No, you don't have to—unless you want the publicity?' Rad challenged.

'It would not be a very . . . nice sort of publicity, would it?'

'No, it wouldn't,' he confirmed evenly. Their eyes met and he added, 'You're going to have a fair amount of it anyway, but I'll go outside just now and tell them you're not speaking to the press.'

'Thank you,' Lesley said levelly. 'You've been helpful, but there's no more you can do now, so you'd better go.'

Rad shook his head. 'Ewart Brummer is on his way over now. I'll wait with you.'

'Why should you?' Lesley bowed her head and went on with faint mockery, 'A man's got to do what a man's got to do, I know. My father deserved to be exposed and all those people he cheated must somehow be compensated, but now I'm thinking of myself . . . The props that have supported me all my life have been taken away, the things I've taken for granted, my parents' money. Even my car will have to be left behind since Daddy registered it in his name, and what will become of my university career? I doubt if I'll get a bursary, and what sort of job can I get without qualifications? You did the right thing, Rad, you did your job and justice will be done because of you, but still I could curse you for what you've done to me.'

'Curse away; it'll make you feel better,' he advised.

'No, I won't give you that satisfaction,' Lesley said resolutely, voice suddenly very clear. 'But oh, I do wonder what's going to become of me!'

CHAPTER THREE

LESLEY no longer questioned Rad's continuing presence in the house. He was there, and she accepted it, and later Ewart Brummer was there too, explaining things to her and helping her to pacify the servants. He and she both provided them with the references her parents had omitted to leave, although, as Ewart said, they scarcely needed them, since the Crosnier staff was renowned and there were many of their northern suburbs acquaintances who had coveted both Lizzy and Absalom. To add to the references he supplied the addresses of a couple of wealthy families who he thought might be glad to pay well for their services.

'Now, Lesley Ann,' he addressed her when that was dealt with. 'I agree with Sinclair that you ought to be out of here by tonight, so I suggest you go and start packing your belongings now. I'll be busy in your father's study for some time yet.'

Rad went away after that, but returned a little later and wandered into Lesley's bedroom.

'How are you getting on?' he asked.

'I've packed my clothes and my textbooks in case some miracle happens and I'm able to return to Varsity next year,' she told him ruefully. 'I'm just wondering how to manage all those.'

He glanced at the array of bottles, tubes and jars littering her dressing-table and smiled sardonically. 'All the tricks of your trade.'

'Trade? Now that's an idea,' Lesley said facetiously.

'Don't be silly,' he retorted quite sharply. 'What about those? They look quite valuable.'

Lesley looked up at the small china items crowding a display structure attached to the wall. 'They are, but they were bought with my parents' money, so they'll be left behind. Every one. For that matter, nearly everything I possess was paid for by my father, but I can hardly go out naked into the world, can I?'

'Not unless you want to pile sensation on sensation,' he agreed, returning to the door. 'I'll be with Brummer. See you later.'

Later, when she had completed her packing, Lesley carried a tray prepared by Lizzy into the study where the men were still busy. Just as she put it down the telephone buzzed and she put out a hand to answer it, but Rad forestalled her. He listened for a few seconds before replacing the receiver gently on its cradle.

Lesley stared at him. 'Abusive?' she whispered.

He nodded grimly. 'Evidently whoever it was hasn't listened to the news bulletins which have reported your father's disappearance.'

Lesley took her own cold drink into the sunroom. It was a stiflingly hot day, but a few members of the press were still coming, and going again without having spoken to anyone other than Absalom, and she had no wish to encounter them. So she remained indoors, trying to make some sort of plan.

It was in the sunroom that Rad found her a little later, and he seated himself in the cane chair opposite her lounger without speaking.

'Ewart still here?' she asked.

'Yes.' He looked at her thoughtfully. 'Well, what have you decided to do?'

'Do?' she queried.

'Where are you going?'

'I haven't decided yet.'

'You've no money, I take it?'

'A few rand.'

'Then you'd better ring one of your boy-friends and ask to be taken in,' he suggested calmly. 'I'm sure such a request would meet with a favourable response.'

Oh yes, she thought, and knew what kind of repayment she would be expected to make for such hospitality.

'No.'

'I was forgetting. They're all ex-boy-friends, aren't they?' Rad taunted. 'What about the new one? Kim Lenny, isn't it?'

'He lives at home with his parents.'

'Who no doubt disapprove of his liaison with you. So what will you do?'

'I'll think of something.' Her smile was very bright.

The smoke grey eyes narrowed. 'You're a brave girl, Lesley Ann Crosnier.'

She tilted her chin. 'I've always been brave.'

'All courage and smiles,' he continued musingly.

'Perhaps this tart has heart too,' she suggested lightly.

'You stand up well under pressure anyway. You haven't shed a tear today, have you?'

'If I wept it would only be for myself,' she told him simply.

'What's wrong with that?'

'Nothing, probably, but tears aren't my way,' she said proudly. 'I know you despise me, Sinclair, but if you're hoping to see me brought that low you'll be disappointed. I will not weep.'

'Perhaps you're incapable of doing so,' Rod mocked. 'There's little emotion in you, is there?'

'Just a sex symbol, that's me,' Lesley agreed flippantly.

'Just a sex symbol, and still practising your smiles when you haven't a clue what you're going to do.'

'I said I'll think of something.'

'I've thought for you,' he told her.

'You have?' She raised her eyebrows carefully. 'Tell me.'

'I've handed over this story and any developments to my junior colleagues and had my leave brought forward,' he explained. 'My best friend in this country owns a citrus farm near Duiwelskloof and there's a sort of rondawel arrangement on the property which belongs to me. I'm going up there tomorrow and I want you to come with me.'

'You're crazy,' Lesley stated coldly.

'Can you suggest a better plan—especially when it would be pleasanter for you to be out of Johannesburg, at least until today's sensation has died down a bit?'

'Remember who caused the sensation?' she said sweetly. 'And yet you expect me to accept this insane invitation to stay in a rondawel with you . . . and share your bed, I suppose?'

'Now you've forgotten something,' Rad suggested impatiently.

'Of course . . . I'm not your type.'

'Right. So you'll stay with Mike and Yolande in their house.'

'I want no favours, nor any charity, Sinclair.' Lesley remained serene. 'Allow me to organise my own life, please.'

'But can you?' He was sceptical.

'Of course,' she smiled.

'Let's see you do it then,' he challenged, standing up.

'Now?' she protested, pouting.

'Now, Lesley. Come on, get on to the telephone and organise your future. On your feet!'

He grasped her arm and jerked her to her feet, propelling her in the direction of the nearest telephone which happened to be in the hall.

'This is unnecessary,' she declared icily.

'No, it's not. Get on with it,' Rad ordered. 'Who's going to take you in? Your godparents?'

'Perhaps.'

'Then phone them.'

'Not with you listening.'

'I'm not leaving you until I know what you've settled,' he stated inexorably, leaning against the wall, obviously prepared for a long wait.

'Damn you,' Lesley said succinctly, and dialled Thelma's number.

Thelma's plummy voice altered perceptibly when she realised who was speaking.

'Oh, it's you, Lesley . . . I was just on my way out, so you'll have to make it quick. What did you want?'

'A favour, Aunt Thelma,' Lesley said blandly, but knowing what the response would be. 'I don't know if you've heard yet that my parents have left the country?'

'I expected it.'

'Yes, well! I've been left holding the baby,' Lesley continued with humour which was an effort. 'I've got to get out of the house and I need somewhere to stay, so I was wondering if you and Uncle William could put me up for a while.'

'I'm afraid not,' Thelma's answer came quickly. 'We leave for Kandersteg in a few days' time and won't be returning until after Christmas.'

'And you don't want a nice clean-living caretaker for your house while you're away?'

'Clean-living?' Thelma could be malicious. 'You must understand, Lesley, that William and I feel very badly let down by these disclosures about your father.'

'I do understand,' Lesley agreed coldly. 'Only too well, Aunt Thelma. I understand that I've become as unacceptable as my parents by virtue of my relationship to them, even though I knew nothing of what my father was up to. I always wondered what my godparents were for. I wonder still more now.'

She put down the receiver without waiting for a response. She felt unable to look at Rad just yet, but she squared her shoulders bravely.

'Who will you try next?' he asked blandly. 'You've no relatives, I take it?'

'No, both my parents were only children.' Lesley thought for a moment. 'Of course, there's my friend Chrissie from Varsity. All is not yet lost.'

Chrissie herself answered, lowering her voice to a breathless whisper when she recognised Lesley. 'Lesley! Oh, poor Lesley, has your father been arrested? What will happen?'

'I don't know yet. You see, he and my mother have skipped the country and I suppose a lot depends on where he turns up and whether that country is prepared to deport him,' Lesley explained.

'And you? What will you do?'

'Why are you whispering, Chrissie?' Lesley met Rad's eyes briefly and he smiled sardonically.

'It's my mother,' Chrissie answered exasperatedly. 'She's impossible today, all I-told-you-so, no-good-will-come-of-it and never-again-will-that-girl-set-foot-in-this-house . . . You know what she's like about you, Lesley.'

'I know. It's a pity, because I was going to ask if I could come and stay with you, but I realise it would be impossible,' Lesley said calmly. 'Never mind, Chrissie, I'll think of something else. I have to leave here, you see. I don't know if I'll be returning to Varsity next year, but either way I'll be in touch with you soon.'

They talked a little longer before ringing off and Lesley turned to Rad with a smile which was only slightly tremulous.

'This is worse than my old scarlet woman image,' she commented.

'You'll meet with the same reaction from most people,' he stated cruelly.

'I still have to try.'

'Why expose yourself to further humiliation? Who else is there?'

To her horror, her mind had gone blank and she couldn't think of a single name. She felt dizzy, light-headed and unbearably tired. For the first time in her adult life, Lesley didn't want to stand alone; she wanted to lean, but she refused to give way to such weakness before this strange, enigmatical man.

'I don't know,' she admitted quietly.

'That settles it, then,' Rad said coolly. 'You'll spend tonight at Heather Louw's flat. I'm due for a final check-up with my doctor early tomorrow morning, after which we'll drive up to Duiwelskloof.'

'No.'

'Yes, Lesley.' He was inexorable.

'No. You've done this to me. I won't go with you!'

'You're not stupid, Lesley, so why give that impression?' Rad demanded impatiently, levering himself away from the wall to grasp her shoulders and shake her. 'You've no alternative and you know it. Can you imagine what it's going to be like for you if you remain in Johannesburg? Most people, lacking your father as a target, are going to focus on you. Not too many will be able to discriminate between the innocent and the guilty. That phone call earlier was just a sample of the foul-mouthed unpleasantness to which sick minds will want to subject you. The press is going to be interested in you, including the Sunday papers. I've already been asked if your life and morals would make an interesting story and I'll bet anything you care to name that your Neville and some of the others have already told their stories to certain reporters. This story will be dragged out and examined from every angle, and anyone who had anything to do with Gerard Crosnier will be of interest, especially his daughter.'

'And all thanks to you.' Her long slanting eyes were hard, but she couldn't hold his gaze and she inclined her head. 'Take your hands off me, Sinclair!'

'With pleasure,' he said urbanely, and did so. 'I'll take you over to Heather's place in a little while.'

'I go consenting.' She raised her head and flashed him her most piquant smile. 'Like the Queen of Sheba, there's no more spirit in me.'

'For the time being,' he guessed drily.

'How is it that you can see me when I can't see you?' Lesley wondered musingly.

'I'm not sure if I understand you.'

'No one does.' She smiled again. 'But you know more than some people.'

'What is there to know, apart from what's already public property?' Rad taunted.

'What, indeed?'

A silence fell between them and Lesley wondered just what further disaster she might be courting in agreeing to go to his friend's farm near Duiwelskloof. He was a stranger as no one else could be a stranger, the one person she had failed to read with her senses. His motives were a mystery and since exposing her father's crimes he seemed to have done a total volte-face in that he was now willing to interest himself in her welfare. Why? When he despised her? Because that was the one thing about him that was clear to her: his contempt.

'Lesley,' he said suddenly.

'Yes?'

'I'm sorry.'

'Why should you be?' she asked mildly. 'I believe in

the press. You did your job.'

'And in so doing, did this to you,' he supplemented harshly. 'I've seen enough of the suffering of innocents the world over, and now I myself have caused an innocent to suffer. Admittedly I couldn't have withheld the story, but I really thought you knew about your father's activities and understood what I was talking about the other night.'

'I can understand that,' Lesley conceded gravely. 'I don't appear as an . . . an innocent sort of person, I know.'

'And after all, it's only in one area of your life that you're lacking in innocence,' he claimed.

'I don't suppose you'd fall for the more sinned against than sinning line,' she suggested, slanting him a provocative glance.

'With those eyes?' he derided. 'No, Lesley, I wouldn't.'

Nor, she knew, would he ever believe the truth about her, that she was innocent in all areas of her life. Only her mind, too easily able to see through to the meagre hearts of those about her, was experienced.

By the time Rad had driven her over to Heather Louw's elegant Killarney flat, Lesley was beginning to feel the strain engendered by the discoveries of the day, and she was relieved when he departed almost immediately after warning her to be ready when he called for her the following day.

No need with Heather, one of the few members of her circle in whom she could perceive nothing but kindness, for smooth smiles and witty remarks. Her quiet company was a balm, and Lesley relaxed a little as she was shown the designer's studio before helping her prepare a light supper.

After the meal they sat in front of the television set,

and when the news came on Lesley buried her face in her hands as a still of her father appeared behind the newsreader.

'Oh, God!'

'I'm sorry, Lesley.' Heather switched the set off. 'I should have realised.'

'So should I.' Lesley was rueful. 'I'll just have to get used to it. After all, I've already had some experience of notoriety.'

'If you want to talk about it, don't feel you'll be embarrassing me,' Heather adjured generously. 'If not, however, I'll keep off the subject too.'

Lesley laughed. 'I want to scream about it, and cry, and curse—and then forget it. But what's to be said? It can't be undone, so I'll just have to live with it and try to accept it, but even my own future is affected by it, so it keeps returning to me.'

'It'll do you good to be at the Wards' farm for a while, I think,' Heather suggested. 'There you won't have it coming at you from all sides, and it's a beautiful old place. I've been there.'

'With Rad?'

'Yes, just for a weekend. Michael and Yolande are darlings and their daughter Shanie is a delight. She worships Rad—and he, I might add, is more indulgent with her than I've ever seen him with anyone.' Heather laughed. 'I sometimes ask him if he's waiting for her to grow up, but he never gives me a serious answer. She'll have just finished school, though, so perhaps I'll get my answer soon.'

From the way Heather spoke so equably about this Shanie, Lesley concluded that her weekend had probably been spent in the Wards' house, not in Rad's rondawel.

'Who is Rad Sinclair, Heather?' she asked softly.

Heather looked perplexed. 'Why, Lesley, you

know who he is.'

'No, I don't.' Lesley shook her head, then hesitated. 'You see, I've got . . . the sight, as I think it's called. Not really, of course, I can't foretell the future or anything, but I feel things. I can . . . sense people, see them clearly underneath the images they're projecting.'

'Now I feel selfconscious!' Heather looked alarmed.

'There's no need,' Lesley laughed reassuringly. 'Everything I see in you is nice. But Rad, now . . . It's the first time it's happened. I can't seem to see him, it's as if he was hidden by a mist, so you see, I need some help.'

Heather shook her head. 'He's on a different plane, Lesley. That's why you can't see him. I don't really know him either. Of course, I've been in love with him for years, like most of the women who know him, but I only know him as he appears. He usually takes me out a few times when he's in South Africa, but he's never taken me into his bed. That's for other women. He likes me, you see, and I'm proud of that and satisfied with it. He's been in some terrible places and seen some terrible things, Lesley, things he'll never talk about, and I suppose his experiences remove him from the rest of us.'

Lesley asked no more, but she wondered at the older girl's calm acceptance of such a state of affairs. Never having been in love herself, she couldn't draw conclusions from personal experience, but it seemed unusual for a woman to love a man and be satisfied with his respect. It probably stemmed from Heather's niceness. Her mother, now . . . Valerie had loved Gerard Crosnier to the exclusion of all else, and had he not loved her in return she would have fought for him. It was love, blind love, which must have made her condone his illegal activities—and Lesley was sure she had been aware of them—and flee South Africa with him without even a thought for her daughter, the product of that love. Valerie's child had been incidental; Gerard was everything to her.

Lesley was still thinking about her parents, and about Rad and Heather, when she fell asleep.

Rad arrived fairly early the next morning, but Lesley and Heather had already breakfasted and the former was ready to leave.

'My God!' Rad said resignedly when he saw her, and turned to Heather. 'She evidently imagines Duiwelskloof is on the coast.'

'I did geography at school,' Lesley assured him, glancing complacently down at her smooth legs below minuscule denim shorts with which she wore a black sleeveless top with a narrow gap dipping down between her firm breasts. She turned round slowly, batting her eyelashes. 'Don't you like it?'

'I like the look of it,' he replied meaningly. 'But the reason for it? Can she possibly be planning to seduce me?'

'It depends. What did your doctor say about your blood-pressure?'

He laughed. 'You're back in form this morning—and what a form!'

'The phoenix rising from the ashes, that's me,' Lesley declared demurely.

'Oh no, Lesley,' Rad shook his head. 'You were never reduced to ashes.'

'I merely tasted them. The ashes of defeat.'

'Nothing could defeat you. Come on, let's get going. It's a longish drive and it's going to be a hot day.'

'Did your doctor say you were fit for a long drive?' Heather asked anxiously.

'Yes, but I'm expecting Lesley to spell me at the wheel.'

'That's all right, then.'

They said their goodbyes, and Lesley watched Rad kiss Heather gently on the cheek and thought pityingly that Heather deserved better.

'How are you feeling today?' Rad asked when they were on the highway between Johannesburg and Pretoria.

'How should I be feeling?' Lesley shrugged gracefully. 'I like your car.'

'It's new.' It was a white Citroën. 'Has the collapse of your world been put behind you already?'

'Isn't that the best way?' she queried lightly.

'You don't hate your parents for what they've done to you?'

'How can I hate, where I never loved?' she challenged with slow thoughtfulness. 'Nor did they love me.'

'Whom have you ever loved, Lesley?' Rad asked mockingly.

'Me, myself and I,' she chanted.

'No one else?' he probed.

'No . . . yes, my granny.'

'She's dead?'

'Yes, my parents killed her,' Lesley said coldly.

'Are you trying to shock me?'

'I couldn't, could I?'

'Well then, stop being so melodramatic and tell me the truth.'

'The truth is that she embarrassed them, so they sent her away to a home where she died of despair and disillusionment.'

'A lot of elderly people are happier in homes than living with their families,' he reminded her mildly.

'Well, she wasn't,' Lesley assured him icily. 'I saw how it changed her. I looked at her and knew she would die. I used to visit her and tell her lies about her dog. They sent him away too . . . I don't know where, but he was an unmanageable animal, so I don't suppose anyone would have given him a home.'

'And is all this history and the obvious lack of parental affection the reason for your sleeping around with all and sundry when you're not yet twenty-one?' Rad asked calmly.

She wondered what he would say if she denied being promiscuous.

'No, I'm not that complex, darling.' She turned her head and smiled at him. 'I thought you'd heard the gossips? I'm a nymphomaniac, remember? Quite insatiable.'

'I remember.'

'And it's got you worried?'

'Well, I do keep getting a glimpse of those beautiful legs,' he retorted. 'Not that I mind, of course. Just as long as you're not contemplating leaping on to me and tearing my clothes off while I'm driving.'

'I'll wait until we're stationary,' she promised liltingly.

'Stopping is forbidden on this highway, more's the pity.'

'The pleasures we have to wait for are the sweetest.'

'Why are you flirting with me?' Rad asked abruptly. 'You weren't yesterday.'

'I flirt with all men,' she said outrageously. 'Yesterday a shock had set me back.'

'But today you're back to normal? Then is this going to be the tone of our entire relationship?' Rad enquired silkily. 'Perhaps you've forgotten the things I said to you the night we met?'

'Dare I hope that you've forgotten them?' Lesley retaliated flirtatiously. 'Since you look like being the only man in my life for a while . . .'

'All right, we'll play it your way,' he said, and there was a distinct threat in his voice. 'But let's both understand a few things first. I don't like you and, you've previously led me to believe, you don't like me. But you're a beautiful woman, Lesley Ann Crosnier. If you throw yourself at me, I'm going to take what's offered. Got that? If you want to continue with this game, carry on as you were. If you want to back out, do so now, and shut up.'

Lesley touched her red lips with the tip of her tongue and surveyed him obliquely in total silence. He was long and lean and strong, totally relaxed and in control as he sat at the wheel in his faded blue jeans and slate grey shirt which revealed muscular, tanned arms and a powerful neck. What was she doing? This wasn't one of the usual young men she could play with and lead on, and still know herself safe from the union which her frigidity made her regard with revulsion. Rad Sinclair was more of a man than those, a hard man who was quite capable of overriding her. 'No, I'm sorry . . .' if she had aroused him sufficiently.

She said very carefully, 'Rad, let's postpone the next round. I know I appear to be back to normal but in actual fact I'm worried sick about my future. I want to get my degree. I keep thinking about that.'

'Then don't,' Rad advised. 'Leave it for a couple of weeks and then come back to the problem.'

'But what am I going to do?'

'We'll think of a solution.'

'I can't think of one, not a single one,' she assured him faintly.

'Then I'll think for you.'

'Why should you?' she asked. 'Come to that, why are you doing this? Why should you do anything for me?'

'Let me be honest, Lesley,' he said thoughtfully. 'I don't think I'd go out of my way to help you, but since I am able to do so and since I did this thing to you . . . Well, why not?'

'Just impersonal help, then. No guilty conscience?'

she queried with an acid little smile.

'None whatsoever,' he agreed blandly. 'Although, as I've said, I'm sorry that you should have suffered.'

'In the cause of truth and justice,' she mocked. 'That's fair enough, darling, but since you dislike me, aren't you concerned that I might ruin your leave for you?'

'I wouldn't let you.'

'How could you stop me?'

'Quite easily,' Rad drawled. 'I'd make you my slave.'

Lesley drew a quiet breath. 'You couldn't, you know.'

'Compliant only in bed, then?'

'And never servile. Anyway,' Lesley altered the subject deliberately, 'what would . . . er . . . Shanie say to such a state of affairs?'

He laughed. 'Do I recognise one of Heather's pet theories? Shanie is . . . just Shanie. She'll know you for what you are, Lesley, but there's no need to give her a detailed account of your chequered career. She's only just out of school, remember.'

'I do have some scruples, you know,' Lesley pointed out coolly. 'If her parents are giving me hospitality, I'm hardly likely to abuse it in such a way, am I? Anyway, it's the men who kiss and tell, not me. I never even talked about such things with Chrissie, although her mother was convinced I was hellbent on converting her to the Scarlet Sorority.'

'Do I detect a note of bitterness?'

'No. Just of amusement. People do mistake me so.'

'I wonder.'

Lesley didn't rise to that and it was a while before either of them spoke again. She noticed that the look of fatigue still lay about Rad's eyes and that once they reached Pietersburg, where they lunched, he made no protest when she offered to drive. The Citroën was a pleasure to handle, but with both schools and universities having closed for the year, the holiday traffic was heavy and she needed to concentrate on what other road-users were doing.

She drove as far as colourful Duiwelskloof itself, when Rad took over again.

'The route gets complicated from here,' he explained. 'But we're nearly there.'

Lesley made no reply and remained silent as they proceeded round afforested hills and through rich valleys. By now she was wondering about the Wards, wondering if they would regard her as a criminal as Thelma and Chrissie's mother had done, and wondering, if they did, how she should react. Bright and defiant? Not humble and crushed anyway. She was guilty of nothing.

'What's wrong?' Rad asked eventually.

'Nothing at all.'

'When you're quiet for as long as this, something is brewing,' he stated confidently.

'I said nothing was wrong,' Lesley enunciated clearly.

'And I say something is,' he retorted, braking and pulling over to the side of the red dirt road on which they were now travelling. He parked in the shade of an ancient bluegum and half-turned in his seat. 'I'm not taking you any farther until I've found out what's troubling you.'

'I'm not myself, that's all,' she said with a quick little smile.

'I can see that.'

'Let's just forget it.' She was unwilling to admit to him, of all people, her sudden fear of meeting these Wards.

Rad looked at her narrowly for a few moments; then he smiled.

'I get it. The addict is missing her daily dose.'

'I suppose you'd like to supply it,' she replied flatly.

'Those legs finally got to me, Lesley.' His eyes lingered on their slenderness, then moved slowly up over her hips to her breasts, and Lesley realised that she was holding her breath.

'You're quite wrong, you know,' she told him levelly.

'I'd like to test the truth of that.'

Now he would find out, she thought a litttle wildly. Already, as Rad drew her across to him, she was stiffening, knowing that she might endure, but never respond.

The touch of his lips was masterly, as she recognised, more expert than other lips which had formerly claimed hers, and he didn't squeeze or grope, but caressed, his hands stroking a rhythmic pattern over her shoulders and back and now down to her thighs. Briefly he raised his head and gave her the strangest look. Then his mouth took hers again.

Lesley's heart was thudding as she lay unyielding against him, feeling the stirring urgency between his thighs. He was different, different, her mind cried. So very different, with his warm, deep kisses, his lips now moving down to the cleft between her breasts.

And still different. Because now he was putting her away from him.

'What's wrong?' they both asked at the same time.

'On this side, nothing, but you, Lesley . . .' He smiled sardonically. 'You weren't exactly resisting me, but neither was I getting any response.'

'You could sense that?' For once she dropped her guard, startled by such a phenomenon.

'Of course I could,' Rad retorted impatiently. 'God, woman, I'm not into necrophilia!'

A fleeting half-smile crossed her face and long lashes swept down over slanting, shadow-green eyes. 'You've just surprised me again, Rad,' she whispered delightedly. 'You're the first man ever to feel that.'

She looked up to see a wicked glint appear in smoky eyes, while his lips quirked.

'Are you telling me that you're always like that?'

'Yes, Rad,' she murmured. 'Congratulations, you're the first to know. I'm frigid!'

CHAPTER FOUR

RAD laughed and laughed.

'It's not that funny,' Lesley pouted.

'It's the funniest thing I've heard,' he retorted. 'Funny and tragic. Woody Allen would love you.'

'And recommend deep analysis.'

' "I'm frigid," she said!' Rad was still laughing. 'Never mind, Lesley, it's a problem we'll overcome—but this is neither the time nor the place.'

He restarted the car and Lesley sat back and relaxed, her anxiety about meeting the Wards forgotten.

'You definitely consider it a problem?' she queried with mock solemnity.

'Certainly. A grave one.'

'A grave . . . social problem?'

'Well, it has affected your social life in a sense, hasn't it?' Rad challenged. 'Presumably you jumped into bed with all those men in an effort to overcome your difficulty?'

'Is that how you see it?' She wasn't ready to tell him the final truth about herself. 'What went wrong, then?'

Rad's amusement disappeared. 'If, as you say, none of them ever noticed your coldness, they were clearly the wrong men.'

'And you're the right one, I suppose?'

'I could be,' he granted blandly. 'As I say, we'll conquer this together.'

'And if I choose not to co-operate?' she asked coldly.

'What have you got to lose? You lost it years ago

and it's a pity to have earned a reputation like yours without deriving any pleasure from the process.'

'Perhaps I'm incurable,' she suggested.

'I refuse to believe it,' Rad stated unequivocally. 'With a body like yours you were palpably meant to be made love to, and enjoy it. Simply, something has frozen you.'

'Perhaps all the attention to my body without ever a thought for my mind and heart,' she tendered sarcastically.

'I've had evidence of the mind, but the heart, Lesley?' His words flicked at her like silken whips. 'Perhaps the lack of it has been the cause of your trouble. I'm the last person to advocate deathless passion, but a little affection can go a long way.'

'Then what's the point of interesting yourself in my problem?' the words glided maliciously out of her. 'There's no love lost between us, is there?'

'Nevertheless, I'd like to try,' Rad countered smoothly. 'I once said you weren't a challenge, but this revelation has made you one. I think I'll make you the grand cause of my leave.'

'A lost cause,' Lesley suggested. 'And not a worthy one either.'

'Perhaps you're right there.'

'What's the idea? Just more of this impersonal help you're willing to tender just as long as you don't have to go out of your way to do so?' she challenged in a tight little voice. 'And when your leave ends you'll tick me off your list as one more good deed done and go on your way.'

'Does the idea worry you?' Rad asked drily. 'It shouldn't. You lack emotion as much as you do physical feeling, so at the end of the course you ought to feel nothing but gratitude. I'll have opened doors for you.'

'Why not go to work on my emotions too?' she taunted.

'No way. Those don't interest me . . . where you are concerned.'

'Nor me.' She slipped in a smile. 'Neither does the other thing, to tell you the truth. So why not just forget it?'

'I can't, now that the matter has been brought to my attention,' Rad informed her suavely. 'However, we can both put it out of our minds temporarily, since we'll be with Michael and Yolande within a few minutes.'

'And Shanie.'

'And Shanie,' he agreed, and Lesley saw his indulgent smile, not for her probing, but for the unknown girl whose image must have come into his mind with the mention of her name.

Michael Ward's great citrus groves lay, rich and healthy, along the valley, and the house was situated a few miles away, on the lower slopes of one of the dark forest-clad hills. The low and the high were separated by a narrow belt of tangled woodland, wild bauhinias, jacarandas and wild pears, above which the old-fashioned house with its red-tiled roof reposed in the midst of a vibrant splash of summer colour. Behind it, the mountains rose, covered by pine and bluegum plantations, dark green and cool-looking in the heat of a still, golden afternoon.

'What am I doing here?' Lesley wondered aloud, voice whimsical. 'And with you? I've got the awful feeling I've run away, but what have I run into?'

'Nervous?' Rad asked, sliding her a quick assessing glance. 'Is that what made you so quiet earlier? No, don't tell me—you're never nervous.'

'Merely wondering how I should react if your friends treat me as my father's partner in crime?

Anyway, do they know I'm coming?'

'They know . . . and they'll treat you as you deserve.'

'That could mean anything,' she protested.

'You had no knowledge of your father's activities,' he stated curtly. 'Therefore they'll treat you accordingly.'

'Because you say so?'

'Because they're that sort of people,' he snapped. 'Did Heather behave as if your company was contaminating her? I choose my friends with greater care than you do, Lesley.'

'I'm sure you do,' she said soothingly. 'I was just wondering, that's all.'

'This is no time to start losing your confidence.'

'I'm not, but you'll admit that it's a little disconcerting to have the only world you've ever known come crashing down and then to be taken among strange people in a strange place,' she suggested. 'I've never been in this area before. The farm is very remote from others, isn't it?'

'Too remote for you?'

'I can't tell yet,' she disclaimed easily. 'I'll try anything once. But for you, after the places you've been in, it must be like . . . oh, like a nice leisurely bath after a long day of hard exercise.'

'Rather more than that,' he said expressionlessly.

'Do you always come here?'

'Yes, when I can manage it, even if it's only for a few days.'

And Lesley wondered if it was his friendship with Michael Ward which brought him here, or the isolation and tranquillity of the beautiful surroundings, or the girl Shanie? Probably a combination, she decided. She still wasn't seeing Rad Sinclair clearly, even after all these hours in his company, but she thought he was too mentally together to be gripped by grand passions. He was a strong man and if, by some remote chance, a magnificent obsession took hold of him, the result would be devastatingly explosive, but that was unlikely to occur.

The garden was a delight. To one side of the house was a swimming-pool, its slate surround scattered with cane chairs and loungers with brightly coloured cushions, and a permanent braai-place on the overlooking top deck, but the rest of the garden rioted profusely as if someone couldn't bear to prune or uproot a single tree or shrub once they had established themselves. Bignonia and its relative, the mauve potato creeper, sprawled lavishly up walls, and Lesley could hardly assimilate the wonderful, vibrant colours of the bougainvillaea; purple clashing exotically with rust, cerise next to gold, lilac, pink, crimson and scarlet, puce and ginger and brick. About a hundred metres away from the house stood a thatched, whitewashed arrangement of two rondawels with a single linking rectangular room, with wax-flowers all about it and shaded by a great old oak.

It was from here that the girl came running as Rad stopped the car in front of the main house and got out. A girl, truly little more than a child, running as fluidly as a gazelle, her long fair hair loose and flying back from her face.

'Rad, oh, Rad!' She came to a halt as she reached him, but the impetus of her rush brought her up against him and she clung to him laughingly as he steadied her. 'I'm so glad, so glad . . . Time went so slowly. I've just been in the rondawels, seeing that everything is just right for you. Oh, Rad, it's been a terrible time! I've kept imagining that your wound might be worse than you'd told us.'

'But now you can see for yourself that I'm still the

man I was,' Rad laughed, brushing a light kiss across her lips and then holding her away from him in order to scan her face. 'All grown up now, Shanie?'

'Well, schooldays are over, but . . . no, not quite grown up yet, Rad.' She giggled and blushed with delightful selfconsciousness. 'I meant to show you, to be all dignified when you arrived, but then I saw you and . . . Oh, Rad!'

She leapt at him and hugged him, and he allowed her a few seconds before putting her gently away from him.

'And you're Lesley Ann?' She turned to their silent, coolly assessing witness and smiled shyly.

She was a slender, dreaming-faced girl with a soft, gentle voice, a dryad who looked as if she might drift vaguely away at any moment. She was a couple of inches shorter than Lesley and her sweet eyes were the same dusky blue as her faded denim jeans.

'She's Lesley,' Rad said with a strange smile. 'Only very occasionally is she Lesley Ann.'

'You're being clever again,' Shanie protested delightedly, and gazed at Lesley again with open admiration. 'Oh, but you're so beautiful!'

Lesley lowered her left eyelid slightly. 'And you, darling,' she said in her best social voice, 'an angel . . .'

'Which Lesley could never be, Shanie,' Rad laughed sardonically. 'So perhaps there's envy flavouring the compliment.'

'I'd rather look like her,' declared Shanie.

'Why, thank you,' Lesley drawled. 'But you wouldn't if you knew how hard I had to work at it.'

Shanie shook her head, apparently missing the inflection of malice. 'No, really, I mean it.'

'This mutual admiration session has lasted long enough,' said Rad. 'Here come Mike and Yolande to break it up, thank God.'

Shanie turned to Lesley with a smile. 'I think men must think only they should pay the compliments, don't you?' she said naïvely.

Lesley responded with a small amused smile. I see you, Shanie Ward, she thought. And wished she could see Rad half as well. As Heather Louw had said, the girl worshipped him, and wasn't she bent on letting him know it! But Rad's feelings in the matter must remain a mystery.

Michael Ward was a stocky, bearded man in his late forties, his wife honey-haired and hazel-eyed and some years younger, with an Afrikaans accent absent in her husband and daughter. They welcomed Lesley kindly and she knew immediately that they did so with complete sincerity.

'Rad says you shared the driving, Lesley, and that you've had no refreshment since stopping in Pietersburg,' Yolande Ward said. 'You must be dying for a drink.'

'She means she's dying for one herself,' Michael teased. 'But come on to the side veranda. We've been expecting you this last half hour, so Johanna will have the ice and everything ready. She and Baptist can attend to your luggage later.'

'I meant to warn you that you'll have to change your habits, Lesley,' Rad remarked when they were all on the shady side veranda overlooking the pool. 'Champagne is for celebrations up here—she's been exclusively a champagne drinker,' he added to Michael.

'Gosh, really?' Shanie was impressed. 'Do you have it for breakfast?'

'We'll really have fallen on decadent times when the Varsity residences serve that for breakfast,' Lesley replied ironically.

'You're a student, then?' queried Yolande. 'But

Michael, why can't we celebrate something if Lesley likes champagne? Rad's safe return to us, for instance?'

'No, please,' Lesley protested. 'As Rad says, I'll have to change my habits.'

'I'm just having orange juice,' said Shanie. 'I don't really like the taste of . . . of drink.'

'Oh, wow!' Lesley said sotto voce and Rad frowned at her.

'You, Lesley?' Michael enquired, sun-tired blue eyes friendly and unjudging.

Lesley surveyed the tray. 'A double tequila and orange, please,' she said clearly.

Rad raised his eyes to the overhanging roof. 'The usual way in company, Lesley, is as a short drink with a lick of salt, and lemon.'

'Oh, let her have what she wants,' Yolande laughed. 'Then I needn't feel guilty at asking for a very, very strong gin and tonic.'

Lesley moved closer to Rad. 'I'm so sorry,' she said quietly, eyes glinting. 'Am I behaving badly?'

'Very.'

'I'm frightened, you see.' Now her voice was a passable imitation of Shanie's.

'Bitch,' he murmured pleasantly. 'But I do believe you. Sit down and relax. Nobody is going to jump up and denounce you, or even say anything tactless.'

He moved away to help his friend with the drinks, and soon they were all sitting down with glasses in their hands and Michael was questioning Rad about his experiences and present state of health.

'But much of it isn't fit for present ears, Mike,' he wound up firmly after a while.

'Meaning me?' Shanie, sitting at his feet, looked up guilelessly.

'Meaning all of you here. You're all too nice to

know what I know.'

'I really ought to experience everything,' Shanie announced next. 'I'm going to be an actress, Rad. I've already been accepted by Wits University Drama Department for next year.'

'Congratulations, that's very ambitious of you,' he said tolerantly, and his eyes gleamed. 'You ought to discuss it with Lesley. She's a very skilled actress.'

'Really?' Shanie was entirely credulous.

'He's joking, Shanie,' Lesley said smoothly.

'What are you studying then?' Michael asked.

'Nothing as ambitious as Drama. Simply, History and English.'

'But you could easily be mistaken for an actress, with your looks,' said Yolande admiringly. 'You know how to use make-up to dramatic effect, your voice is beautiful and you're so poised and slim . . . I keep looking at you and Shanie and thinking—I was like that once. Sylphlike.'

'And look at her now,' Michael laughed affectionately.

'She's just the way you like her, Mike,' said Rad. 'And she knows it.'

'Plump, just a little plump,' Yolande bemoaned.

'If you will sample your own cooking, darling!'

Yolande looked at Lesley. 'I have Johanna to clean the house, but I do all the cooking, Lesley. I'm a housewife by choice. It's all I've ever wanted to be.'

'Then it's what you were born to be, Yolande,' Rad said indulgently. 'But I doubt if Lesley can understand something like that.'

'Au contraire,' Lesley retaliated with a wide beautiful smile. 'I understand Mrs Ward very well. You've found your own space where you're needed and you don't covet anyone else's, do you?'

'I just covet their figures,' Yolande laughed. 'Yes,

Lesley, that's about it, and since you understand me so well, you'll have to call me Yolande.'

'Thank you.'

Lesley thought of what Rad had said about choosing his friends with care. Her highly sensitive mind had already imbibed the essence of this family. She liked Yolande with the honey-coloured knot at the nape of her neck slipping rapidly into disorder, and too she liked fair Michael of the quiet voice and weather-toughened skin. As for Shanie—she saw and understood her too, even if she didn't like her.

It was Shanie, a little later, who slipped away briefly and then returned to say, 'Johanna has taken your cases up to your room, Lesley. Wouldn't you like to unpack now? I could help you. I'm dying to see your clothes. I'm sure someone like you has tons of wonderful things.'

'Don't feel obliged to give her anything she takes a fancy to, Lesley,' Yolande warned as she stood up. 'I know to my cost what my daughter can achieve with a wistful look!'

'I doubt if Shanie and I share many tastes,' Lesley said ambiguously.

'Lesley never gives anything away,' Rad said even more ambiguously as he stood up. 'Come over to my place with me, Mike. I'll see you when I come over for dinner tonight, Lesley. Until then, behave yourself.'

'Why did he say that?' Shanie asked breathlessly as she escorted Lesley upstairs.

'Perhaps he thinks I'll be a bad influence on you.'

'Because you're a . . . a siren type?' Shanie wondered. 'But I'm sure you're very nice underneath, Lesley.'

'And I'm sure you're incorruptible, angel,' Lesley returned wickedly.

'Oh, but I'd love to be corrupt,' Shanie insisted with

engaging youthfulness. 'Well, perhaps not corrupt, but sort of decadent and slinky and sophisticated.'

'Like me?' Lesley was longing to laugh.

'Yes, that's exactly it,' Shanie breathed. 'D'you think you could improve me while you're here; you know, make me over?'

'You're perfect as you are for the time being,' Lesley said lightly, and it was the truth.

The room Shanie took her to was spacious and contained some beautiful old-fashioned furniture, including a high wide bed, while a vast window stood open to a view of dark green hills, just the tops of the trees glinting gold in the sunlight.

'Do you really want to help me unpack?' Lesley enquired sceptically of her companion.

'Oh, yes!' Shanie was ludicrously fervent.

And she exclaimed rapturously over each and every garment that emerged from Lesley's cases, and wanted to experiment with her make-up there and then.

'I only wear a little lip-gloss, eye-shadow and mascara, and not always. I'm such a safe sort of person, you see,' she confided.

'You don't need anything at all,' Lesley assured her.

'I feel I do. I want to be the sort of woman Rad will admire,' Shanie stated frankly. 'He must think you're wonderful, to have brought you here with him.'

'He thinks nothing of the sort,' Lesley said clearly. 'He despises me, and if you start imitating me . . . well, I dread to think!'

'Oh no, I'm sure he adores you,' Shanie insisted.

It was like having a chattering child with her, Lesley thought, a child too young to be reasoned with. She surveyed the girl now sitting at the dressing-table in silence for a while, then said blandly:

'You're not for real, are you, Shanie Ward?'

Shanie looked startled, twisting round to stare up at

her with bewildered eyes. 'I'm sorry,' she murmured politely. 'I don't understand?'

Lesley shrugged. 'Forget it.'

Shanie instantly did so. 'You must have masses of boy-friends, Lesley. I haven't any.'

'You will have.'

'There's only one man I want,' Shanie brought out candidly. 'And to him I'm just a child. I know he's probably in love with you, or Heather Louw, or even one of the ones who've stayed in the rondawel with him ... when I've been away at boarding-school, those, but I get to hear of them.'

'He's probably in love with you and waiting until you're old enough for him to ...' Lesley played up to her mischievously. 'What's the phrase? Declare himself. Perhaps he's even spoken to your parents about it.'

'Oh, do you really think so?' Shanie gave no indication that she suspected teasing. 'You must be so experienced, Lesley. Tell me about your boy-friends.'

'Ah.' Lesley grew very still, and her eyes glowed greenly. 'What shall I tell you about men that you need to know, Shanie? If ever a man breaks your heart, hurts you in any way, think of me and be comforted. I shall have avenged you. I make fools of men, you see.'

Shanie looked perplexed. 'Because they all fall in love with you?'

'Because they all want me,' Lesley moved to where she could see herself in the dressing-table mirror. 'And I despise them. For every one nice man like your father, there are a hundred of the other sort ... And that's my mission in life, melodramatic as it sounds. I take revenge on behalf of womankind. They go away and I laugh at them, and when I hear the lies they're spreading about me, I laugh still more. They're such small, stupid people.'

'You're joking, aren't you?' Shanie was shocked.

'No.' The strange mood had passed, but Lesley was honest.

'I'm sure you're not really like that.' Shanie smiled tentatively. 'I mean . . . Lesley! You wouldn't do such a thing to Rad, would you?'

Lesley smiled delicately. 'Could I?'

That had her worried, she thought complacently, and strolled away to hang another dress in the wardrobe.

'Oh, Lesley, I'm sure you don't really mean it,' Shanie said with sweet determination. 'You're too lovely to think so evilly. You just . . . I know what it is! Someone has hurt you badly and you're still feeling raw.'

Lesley sucked in her cheeks to prevent a smile more spontaneous than those she was accustomed to give. She hadn't enjoyed herself so much for quite a while.

'What a generous person you are,' she cooed. 'Making excuses for me.'

'I hate to think badly of anyone.'

'I can see that. And tell me, do you never feel anger, never raise your voice?'

'I try not to,' said Shanie, apparently believing she was being taken seriously. 'I do try to be a better person than I am, you see, so I must think positively. Oh, Lesley, I'm glad you've come here. I'll leave you alone now because I'm sure you're feeling overwrought after the terrible events of yesterday, and in need of some solitude . . . But I hope we'll be friends. You really must take me in hand and help me improve my appearance, and perhaps I could help you in return, if only by listening to you. Talking might exorcise the bitterness you must be feeling to want to revenge yourself on all men.'

'Perhaps it's only yesterday's traumatic events embittering me,' said Lesley, just to frighten her, as she moved out of the room. 'And only one man on whom

I'll take revenge.'

But Shanie was sworn to think no ill of her. 'Words, Lesley,' she claimed dismissively, and drifted away, smiling vaguely.

Lesley went over and shut the door, then returned to sit on the bed, her expression thoughtful yet amused.

The girl was incredible, she thought. Did she really expect people to be deceived by such a ham performance? And were people in fact taken in?

Lesley could hardly believe it. Even without her ability to see through to the self-absorbed core of the girl, she could not have taken her seriously. No eighteen-year-old could be that naïve. I see you, Shanie Ward, she thought again, just as she had done earlier. Soft and sweet, gentle-voiced and slightly vague, with never a cruel word escaping her rosebud lips, yet Shanie deceived. There was never a moment when she wasn't conscious of self, of Shanie.

Amateurishly over the top as her performance had been, she would probably make a good actress one day. As with all jobs which must be done in the public eye, the stage required a certain amount of egocentricity, and that Shanie had in abundance.

Lesley wondered how her own performance had measured up. The tequila had been talking, she realised now, and felt regretful. She hadn't been as cool as usual and had probably betrayed too much of herself.

She dressed for dinner with her usual care that night and went downstairs in a skimpy drift of scarlet chiffon, with a trio of tiny, artificial scarlet roses among her dark curls, which were shining and scented and arranged in a new style. Rad, with Shanie in softest blue and clinging to his arm, was at the foot of the stairs, having come into the hall by the front door.

They both watched her descent in a silence which paid tribute to both her natural assets and her artifice, and she looked back at them, exotic, frivolous creature of a thousand smiles and wiles.

'Oh, Lesley!' Shanie rhapsodised. 'How divine you look! I could never feel confident in such a vibrant dress . . . not until I've discovered my personality, anyway. I was just telling Rad about how I'm trying to find myself.'

'How fashionable of you to be engaged in such a search,' Lesley complimented her facetiously.

'Obviously you've already found your true self,' Shanie went on, unruffled.

'I never lost myself,' Lesley retorted. 'I've always known exactly who and what I am.'

'But not where you're going, I rather think,' Rad drawled.

'I know where you think I'm going. It's warm there, isn't it?'

'More than. But where you're going right now is into the lounge with Shanie and me where we'll join Mike and Yolande in a drink,' he said urbanely.

Shanie skipped ahead of them like a child, but Rad paused to take hold of Lesley's chin with long cool fingers.

'What an incredible woman you are,' he murmured, eyes on the scarlet curve of her mouth. 'Where you're concerned, it ought always to be night and an occasion for dressing up!'

'A lady of the night?' Lesley suggested gently with a mysterious smile.

'Or a very shady lady.'

'I thought only Heather Louw was a lady, anyway.'

'True.' His eyes dropped to the exquisite swell of her breasts. 'How appropriate the colour, darling.'

'Why deceive?'

'When did you last wear white?'

'I forget,' she said lightly. 'White and the pastels are for girls like Shanie.'

'She appears to admire you, heaven help her.'

'I adore her already.' Lesley's tone was deliberately false.

Rad's grey eyes were lit with sceptical amusement. 'You do?'

'Who could fail to? Only Rad . . .' she paused delicately. 'If she says "Oh, Lesley" to me once more, I might be so crude as to scream.'

'Oh, Lesley,' Rad echoed tauntingly, putting a hand to her back and propelling her into the lounge.

For the sake of Michael and Yolande who had taken her into their home without question or comment, Lesley muted her act that evening, subduedly playing the rôle of an observer, witnessing Rad's indulgence with Shanie and wondering what his feelings were, if any.

It could indeed be that he was waiting for the girl to grow up. But Shanie was adult now, if only she would drop that ridiculous pose of beguiling innocence. It was no crush she had on Rad, but a woman's determination to win her man. Unlike Heather Louw, she was not prepared to accept their present relationship, but, Lesley thought, she was going about altering it in entirely the wrong way . . . Unless Rad, after the harsh experience he had of the world, found such quaint charm refreshing; and the girl was lovely to look at, with her ethereal fairness and dreaming face.

Occasionally during dinner and after, Rad glanced Lesley's way, but for her his look was never indulgent. Amusement, contempt and derision were all that she merited from him. 'I don't care,' she mouthed the words at him when his look challenged her. And at least it made a change from the open lust with which most men looked at her.

Later on in the evening, returning from a trip to renew her make-up, Lesley once more found herself alone in the hall with Rad, and noticed anew the tiredness marking the area surrounding his eyes, which looked almost black now, while his attractive mouth was tighter than usual.

'You're still not fully fit yet, are you?' she questioned him.

He looked at her in a somewhat reserved way. 'I'll survive.'

'All today's driving must have tired you,' she went on, still studying him. 'You ought to sleep.'

'I don't want solicitude from you, Lesley,' he snapped.

Her eyes widened. 'May I not show a little concern after your . . . kindness?'

'My kindness?' Rad tested the word curiously.

'In doing this for me; bringing me here.'

'I took no trouble over you,' he reminded her cruelly.

'Nevertheless, you brought me along. You needn't have done that.' She paused, searching for words since honesty came to her only with difficulty. 'I do realise what hell it would have been for me to remain in Johannesburg just now.'

'For pity's sake!' He was impatient, close to losing his temper.

'Please,' Lesley appealed quietly. 'I merely wanted you to know of my gratitude, but you make it very difficult for me. For once I'm being honest——'

'And I don't recognise you, Lesley,' he interrupted coldly.

She shrugged philosophically. 'Back to normal, then, but you really ought to sleep now, Rad.'

He smiled drily. 'Well, I won't be doing that just at once. I've a date with Shanie. We're going to take a stroll round some old haunts in the garden and beyond.'

'All under the moonlight? How very romantic!'

Michael and Yolande appeared in the hall at that moment. They had not caught Lesley's words, but her tone had registered.

'A quarrel?' Michael enquired concernedly.

'Far from it, Mike,' Rad laughed, but the look he gave Lesley was inimical. 'Lesley Ann has just been expressing her gratitude to me for bringing her here.'

'However, he appears to have a violent aversion to being thanked,' Lesley supplemented in a cool little voice, the words falling from her red lips like tinkling drops of crystal water. Her smile encompassed both husband and wife. 'I hope you're not the same? Because I do want to thank you both, very much, for allowing me to come into your home like this.'

'Oh, I love gratitude,' Yolande declared, touching her arm in rare understanding. 'But think nothing of it, Lesley. If Rad wants you here, that's good enough for us.'

But perhaps he no longer wanted her here, Lesley thought later that night when she lay wakeful in the strange bed. That last encounter in the hall had found him more hostile to her than she had previously known him, and she wondered what had happened to make him so.

Johanna, the Wards' Lovedu domestic, brought her coffee in bed the following morning. After she had drunk it, Lesley lay back against the pillows. Johanna had drawn back the curtains and from her present position she could see the tops of trees on the hills being stirred by a light breeze.

There was a knock at the door and before she could

voice an enquiry as to who was there, it had swung open and Rad, in inevitable jeans and a casual black-and-gold checked shirt, stepped into the room.

One horrified gasp of recognition, and Lesley had whipped the covering sheet up, right over her head. However, it wasn't her scanty night attire that prompted her action, although her nightdress was a mere wisp of filmy nylon, as scarlet as the dress she had worn the night before, since she was used to displaying a great deal of her beautiful body in company.

'Get out of here,' she instructed him clearly.

'What in the world is wrong with you this morning?' Rad sounded impatient.

'Nothing,' Lesley said sharply. 'Only get out, get out!'

'No, I damn well won't—at least, not until I've discovered what's causing you to behave in this crazy way,' he snapped.

'Go away,' Lesley ordered insistently.

She heard the door close but knew he hadn't left the room.

'Uncover your face, Lesley,' he said calmly.

'No!' Her heart was thumping madly with real panic. 'Nobody, Rad, but nobody sees me without my make-up!'

CHAPTER FIVE

THERE was a brief silence in the room, then Lesley heard Rad approaching the bed.

'That's insane!'

'It isn't,' Lesley said desperately. 'Please, Rad, just go away.'

'No.' She felt the bed take his weight as he sat down on the edge. 'You've intrigued me now, so I'm not leaving this room until you've revealed yourself.'

'I told you, nobody sees me like this.'

'All your lovers, Lesley?' Rad derided. 'Don't tell me they wake up beside you in the mornings to find you already in full warpaint!'

'Yes . . . no! Oh, please,' Lesley begged.

The sheet was wrenched away from her clutching fingers and the next moment he had hold of her wrists and was pinning her arms back against the pillows.

Lesley felt naked as she encountered his searching scrutiny. Helplessly, she lay looked up at him, her lips quivering, while her long green eyes were darkened by uncertainty and self-doubt.

Rad's enigmatical gaze roved over her straight nose and high cheekbones, assimilating the exquisite creamy pallor of her flawless skin, and she saw a strange smile pass over his face.

'Why, you're just a scared little scrap without your mask to hide behind,' he commented musingly. 'But in heaven's name, how can a few smudges of artificial colour become such a vital prop to anyone?'

'I'll never forgive you for this, Rad Sinclair!' Lesley swore with trembling intensity. 'Never, never, never!'

'This is the worst thing I've done to you, seeing you like this?' he questioned her disbelievingly.

'Yes! Oh, I hate you!'

'Talk about unbalanced!' His eyes still moved over her face. 'Don't look so stricken, Lesley—You're still a beautiful woman, even without your make-up . . . So beautiful that I think I'd like to proceed with lesson number one of the course now, while you're in this vulnerable state.'

Her wrists were released and he traced the line of one high cheekbone lightly with his fingers. Lesley continued to look up at him, experiencing an odd fluttering sensation below her ribs. His fingers moved round the rim of her ear, along her smooth jaw and down the side of her neck.

'No,' she said numbly, trying to shake her head, and her lustrous dark curls rippled against the patterned peach and white pillowcase.

'But yes.' Rad's voice contained a slight huskiness and he bent to touch her lips with his, the merest touch only.

'No,' Lesley repeated more insistently.

'Relax, my lovely,' he urged, still bending over her.

'I can't.' For some reason she wanted to weep.

'Relax,' he said again, compelling voice lulling her into obedience. 'It will be all right, I promise you. I won't do anything you don't want me to.'

Lesley remained still as his mouth covered hers, warm and insistent. His arms slid beneath her body, gathering her closer to him as he murmured encouragement between kisses.

And then Lesley felt it, the inner stirring she had never experienced before. It was a mere quivering at first, then a shudder shook her as if some barrier had suddenly given way. She felt as if she was dissolving, deliquescent, and involuntarily she slid her arms up until she could wind them tightly about his neck. Tentatively at first she began to respond to Rad's kisses and then, as he grew more passionate, so did she, her fingers digging into his shoulders as she clung to him.

It was all so new, like being born, and she sighed into his mouth as the wonder of it shook her. He was lying across her by now, but as his lips slid down from her mouth to the hollow at the base of her throat he drew back a little. Somehow the covering sheet and single light blanket were no longer between them and he began to caress her body with long, stroking movements. The touch of his fingers burned through her thin nightdress and she felt her body coming vibrantly to life, for the first time ever, every nerve-end suddenly pulsating with sensitive awareness.

Only when Rad would have slid his hands beneath her nightdress did Lesley shrink from him, afraid of such intimacy, and he gave way to her unspoken wish at once.

'Enough for now?' He moved away from her until he was sitting on the edge of the bed again. Then he bent to kiss her just once more and her lips moved involuntarily against his. 'But you see, Lesley, it wasn't so bad after all, was it?'

But Lesley could only stare up at him in silence. Her cheeks were faintly flushed, rare tears stood in her shadow-green eyes and she swallowed painfully. She felt more frightened than she had ever done in her life; not of Rad but of herself and of the person she would henceforth be. It was as if a room in which she had hidden had been unlocked and the key taken away; she would never feel secure again. Rad had brought her to life—and made her vulnerable.

'And I'll never forgive you for that either,' she declared in a small clear voice, silvery with hatred.

Rad's eyes narrowed. 'May I know why?' he asked chillingly.

'Damn you!' She faltered, searching for words. 'I . . . I didn't want that, I didn't need it.'

'I beg to differ.' Now scorn characterised his tone, terrible searing scorn which caused her to flinch. 'You chose your life-style long ago; now you might as well start getting some pleasure out of it.'

'You don't understand,' Lesley whispered.

'I understand only too well,' he lashed her. 'I never thought you of all people would prove to be a coward, Lesley Ann. I've started the thaw for you and now you're frightened; you'd have preferred to stay safely encased in ice for the rest of your life, wouldn't you? Frigid, joyless—and safe! Safe from pleasure. That's how you wanted to be, and I've ended that for you by making you aware of your capacity for enjoyment.'

It was so close to the truth that Lesley couldn't speak for a few moments. All she wanted at this moment was to bring an end to this scene. That done, she could set about putting it out of her mind as well and doing her best to become again the always-in-control girl she had been.

She sighed, and for the first time since his entry into her room, she attempted one of her smiles, but it emerged as a fragile, flickering thing and she was unable to sustain it.

'You're probably right, Rad,' she conceded wearily. 'But it just so happens that I was content with my life as it was . . . I liked the way I was.'

'No sense of adventure,' he mocked, shaking his head. 'Your life could be so much enhanced; your affairs could take on an altogether richer quality.'

'Possibly.' She closed her eyes briefly and opened them again to find him scrutinising her intently. 'All the same, Rad, I'd rather stay as I was, thank you, so I'd appreciate it if you gave up this idea of . . . of changing my life for me. One lesson was enough.'

'It's too late, Lesley,' Rad warned her. 'I've started this and I intend finishing it.'

'How?'

'Haven't you guessed?' He smiled slightly. 'Whatever I may have said about you, whatever I may still think about you, I happen to want you.'

'Not me. My body.'

'Your beautiful body,' he agreed, and now there was a glint of cruelty in his smoke-coloured eyes, a terrrible detached cruelty which shrivelled Lesley. 'Why the resentment? You know what you are and must expect to be used as such.'

'Used! Yes!' Lesley struggled into a sitting position and her eyes were flashing. 'I know what I am, as I've always known—a commodity.'

'Oh, poor Norma Jean,' Rad taunted.

'I really feel for that woman,' she flared. 'Even after her death they still went on exploiting her.'

'You needn't worry about the same thing happening to you,' he derided. 'Beautiful as you are, you haven't Monroe's impact. Besides, her tragedy was that she yearned to be taken seriously. You've never pretended to be other than what you are.'

'Which is?' Lesley sounded, and felt, icy now.

'I've said the word to you before and you haven't denied it,' he reminded her softly. 'A tart, Lesley. There are other words too, but that will serve.'

'And even despising me thus, you'll make use of me simply for your own fleeting pleasure.'

'I've learnt to accept what's available in the way of women,' Rad told her brutally. 'I've been in parts of the world where I've had to endure weeks or even months without a woman, sometimes without even sight of a woman . . . But why the bitterness, my sweet Lesley Ann? Judging by the crowd of ex-lovers present the night we met, you've never been exactly selective about whom you slept with . . . And if I succeed in melting the last vestiges of your frigidity, you'll have a damned good reason for granting me access to your body. However, you can relax for now. We've plenty of time ahead of us——'

A knock on the door interrupted him and with real gratefulness, Lesley called, 'Come in, please.'

Shanie, in jeans and a T-shirt, entered with a smile on her face, then halted when she saw Rad.

'Oh . . . Rad?' She was disconcerted and her flush of embarrassment was enchanting. 'I've . . . I've interrupted. I'm so sorry, I'll go away again.'

'Please stay,' Lesley inserted coolly before Rad could speak.

'Yes, don't run away, Shanie,' he seconded as he stood up. 'I came to tell Lesley we'd go riding together after breakfast, but I got somewhat sidetracked.'

His amused glance challenged Lesley, but she refused to react and transferred her attention to Shanie, who was now expressing disappointment.

'Oh, dear! I wanted to take her riding myself, Rad. I'm dying to show her over the farm and I thought we could even go up into the hills.'

'We'll all three of us ride,' Rad said indulgently. 'You do ride, Lesley?'

'I haven't for a few years, but like most little girls, I went through a horsey stage and took lessons,' she said ruefully.

'That's settled, then. Come on, Shanie, we'll go away and give her a chance to get up.' He had his arm about Shanie's shoulders and was turning her in the direction of the door. 'See you later, Lesley.'

As soon as they had gone Lesley got out of bed and went into the room's adjoining bathroom, determinedly avoiding catching a glimpse of herself in any mirrors, sure that if she did so and met her own eyes she would feel warm colour rushing into her cheeks. She stripped and stood under the shower, and the cool water running over her body made her feel more like herself and presently she was able to set her thoughts in order.

Why should Rad Sinclair, the one man she had failed to read like a book, also be the one man to have woken her from the frozen sleep of frigidity?

There was no answer to that, so she discarded the question and turned her attention to the future. If Rad lost interest in her or decided that he would rather be entertained by Shanie during his leave, which was quite possible, then she had nothing to worry about. If, on the other hand, he continued to pursue the course he was presently intent on, then she supposed she would have to tell him the truth about herself.

And he would never believe her.

He had charged her with promiscuity too often and never heard an outright denial of it. And yet somehow she would have to convince him, because of all the men in the world, he was the one she was least prepared to have making cynical use of the body he desired even while he despised the woman to whom it belonged, despised what she had allowed him to believe she was.

Least of all, him. She was certain of that, yet unsure of the reason. It had nothing to do with resentment against him for what he had done to her father. Rather, it seemed, she was frightened of him—because he was one whose nature she couldn't see clearly. Not that she needed to know much where she herself was concerned. His feelings comprised solely contempt for her and desire for her body. There was nothing more. Yet Lesley was sure that behind the mist which hid him from her, he was a highly complex man, too complicated for her, and yet clear-cut too, because everything about Rad Sinclair was positive.

'To hell with him!' Lesley whispered aloud, and practised a dismissive smile as she stepped out of the shower. She was sufficiently recovered to be able to face her lovely, mirror-reflected image without blushing.

Lesley rode with Rad and Shanie that morning, and most mornings after that, on the fairly good horses that Michael Ward kept out in an open field above the house. They were pleasant enough rides and she still found Shanie amusing. Additionally, she had come to appreciate the beauty of this area to which Rad had brought her. In these long, still days of a searingly hot summer, the strong, clear colours she loved abounded; the dark green of the afforested hills, the scarlet of poinsettias, the magnificent clash of different coloured bougainvillaea, the luxuriant orange groves and the red roads between.

Sometimes she saw Rad in the afternoons, other times not, and once she had heard the sound of a typewriter being used in his rondawel cottage. When she did see him it was because he joined her and Shanie in or beside the swimming pool.

The first time Lesley saw the scar of the healed bullet wound in his left shoulder, a strange weakening sensation swept through her. Forgetful of the coolly detached image she was striving for, she stared at it with eyes glazed with horror.

Then she lifted her gaze to Rad's face and encountered a sardonically amused smile.

Shanie was kicking about in the deep end of the pool, heedless of them both for the moment, and Rad strolled over to where Lesley was relaxing on a lounger.

'What does that look signify?' he wondered tauntingly. 'Revulsion or pity?'

Lesley picked up her sunglasses and put them on quickly. 'Which would you prefer?'

'Neither,' he laughed shortly. 'I'd prefer you to overlook it.'

'It's hardly unnoticeable,' Lesley said maliciously.

'You'll give me a complex yet!'

She smiled delicately at that. 'I don't believe it. You're not a narcissistic man, Rad.'

'Whatever else I may be?' he challenged.

'I didn't say that,' she reminded him amicably.

'Your tone did,' he countered. 'It, and your smile, suggested a whole list of character flaws you could enumerate if you chose.'

'But I don't choose, darling,' Lesley returned sweetly. 'It would hardly be . . . dignified to resort to a slanging match.'

'How wise of you.' Rad was now occupying the lounger beside hers, and he had his head turned slightly so that he could continue looking at her. His eyes narrowed slightly. 'Or could it be that you're afraid of my returning the compliment and presenting you with a similar list?'

'Not at all,' Lesley denied calmly, stretching out an arm and examining her long, pearlised red nails. 'I know myself, Rad.'

'I doubt it,' he said abruptly.

A silence fell and, concealed by dark lenses, Lesley's eyes returned to his scarred shoulder as if hypnotically compelled.

'Stop it,' he snapped, no longer looking at her but watching Shanie, who was performing a series of graceful movements which had some similarity to water-ballet.

'Stop what?' Lesley asked softly.

'I don't even need to see you to know what you're

looking at,' Rad elaborated impatiently, and she was surprised at his ability to sense such a thing. 'What is this—some sort of morbid fascination with ugliness?'

'It's not ugly,' she contradicted him, then added honestly, 'Or it won't be. It's healing nicely. But it must have been a hell of a mess at the time, Rad.'

'It was,' he conceded expressionlessly, and now his face was inscrutable, and Lesley knew that he had slipped back in time and place to that seething little state where opposing fanatics had stopped at nothing to put power in the hands of whichever despot they had happened to support.

'It must have been painful.'

'Now you're being fatuous,' Rad scorned.

'Yes, I am,' she agreed apologetically. 'It's just that when I remember where you've been and what you've seen, I feel at a loss. You know Real Life with capital letters; I don't.'

'I also know how cheaply life is regarded in so many parts of the world,' he replied drily. 'Reality is everywhere, Lesley, not just in violence and war, and suffering is relative.'

'That's a tolerant view.' She was curious about him. 'Then do you value life?'

'Why else would I do what I do?' He was dismissive, and she sensed that he wished to close the discussion, but she persisted, needing to know more about him since her sensitive mind had failed her where he was concerned.

'Meaning that if enough people can be shocked by the truth, there might be an end to the . . . horror?'

'"The horror . . . the horror", as Kurtz, either Conrad's or Coppola's, would have it.' Rad shook his head. 'You take a simplified view, Lesley. Enough people . . . Most people are too absorbed in contending with their own realities to do more than simply be aware of other people's, save one or two, perhaps. Those one or two will be enough for me. But this is getting too earnest. Change the subject.'

'In a moment,' she said quietly. 'One last question, though: is that wound still painful?'

'And what a womanly question it is,' he laughed, standing up. 'No, Lesley. Apart from the occasional muscular stiffness, I no longer feel it, so you needn't refer to it again.'

Lesley watched him stroll away from her to join Shanie in the pool. She wondered why he had such an aversion to any comment about his wound. It wasn't selfconsciousness that was the cause, so she supposed it must be an unwillingness to remember too often the danger he had faced and would face again. He had admitted that he valued life, and that would include his own life, but he had a job to do and thinking too often of the risks it entailed would render it intolerable.

She watched his long, powerful body cleaving through the water. Clearly the wound no longer hampered him physically. He was virile and tanned, essentially masculine, and for a moment Lesley could feel again his lips on hers, the weight of his body crushing her . . . But she was strong-willed enough to discard the memory.

Her eyes turned again to the scar-tissue marking his gleaming brown shoulder, and a feeling of poignant regret surprised her. When his leave was over, Rad would return once more to the trouble-spots of the world, to walk again the road of danger, facing further injury and perhaps even death. She wondered if he would ever think of her when he was gone. Somehow she doubted it.

'Your mouth has a sad droop to it this afternoon, Lesley.' Yolande Ward had come outside and now she lowered herself on to the lounger Rad had been occupying.

Instantly Lesley turned on a bright self-mocking smile. 'Your kindness and the beautiful surroundings must be causing me to relax a little too much, Yolande. I don't usually forget to control my facial expressions.'

'You do so love to project a certain image, don't you?' Yolande's hazel eyes went to the couple in the pool, and she sighed. 'So does my daughter. Why can't people be natural?'

'Perhaps we need to have achieved happiness as you have done before we can let it all hang out,' Lesley suggested thoughtfully.

'But at twenty and eighteen respectively, you and Shanie ought to be strangers to unhappiness,' Yolande protested.

'I'm not saying we're actively unhappy,' Lesley assured her quickly. 'But your kind of happiness is total. That's why you and Michael are . . . completely natural. Neither of you dissembles. For Shanie, as for me, I suppose, uncertainties exist.'

'To be young is to be frightened,' Yolande agreed with a smile. 'What are you scared of, Lesley?'

'Of being seen to be scared,' Lesley confessed with difficulty. No one but Yolande could have won such an admission from her.

'And Shanie?'

Lesley was silent. She understood Shanie too well, but this was the girl's loving mother questioning her and she liked Yolande enough to allow her to retain her illusions about her daughter.

'Of . . . not winning,' she said eventually, as honestly as she could.

'Yes.' Yolande sighed again. 'She's such a very silly little girl at times, but oh, she's so very much in love with Rad, and I don't want her to be hurt.'

'Perhaps she won't be.'

'You mean . . . oh, Lesley, I hardly think so.' Yolande shook her head and a few gleaming strands of hair slipped from the knot at the nape of her neck. 'She's far too immature to hold much appeal for Rad.'

'She's pretty and whimsical and as elusive as a creature from the spirit world,' Lesley said guardedly. 'It could be that after some of the places he's been in, Rad finds her freshness and simplicity a welcome change.'

'Those last two qualities add up to naïveté, I'm afraid,' Yolande disagreed. 'If she wasn't so childish . . . that's why I'm glad of your presence, Lesley. Coming into daily contact with you, Shanie may come to realise that it requires more than girlish charm to interest a real man. If Rad would just show her that he prefers the sophisticated woman to the ingénue, she'd drop this ridiculous act, and that would be all to the good, whether she finally wins him or not.'

Lesley shook her head smilingly. 'I'm afraid that's one thing he won't show her, Yolande. Other sophisticated women, yes—but never this one.'

Lesley was not alone with Rad again until after she had been five days on the Wards' farm, and even then Baptist, the middle-aged black man who looked after the garden in a haphazard way when Yolande could bring herself to give him orders, was weeding not far away from where she lay beside the pool.

Rad wasn't clad for swimming when he joined her. Instead, he wore grey jeans and a cream shirt which was left hanging open to reveal his bronzed chest with its covering of fine dark hairs.

'Where is Shanie this afternoon?' he asked.

Lesley discarded the day-old newspaper she had been studying. 'Yolande had driven her in to Tzaneen or Duiwelskloof . . . I'm not sure which. She wanted to have her hair cut.'

Rad raised his eyes to the burnished blue heavens. 'Just like Lesley Ann's, I suppose?'

'I think we dissuaded her from that,' Lesley replied complacently. 'After all, she must develop her . . . individual personality.'

'Bitch,' he commented pleasantly. He glanced down at the newspaper. 'How's the world?'

'Still turning.' Lesley touched her upper lip with the tip of her tongue. 'My parents still haven't been located by either the press or certain other people who are looking for them. I guess they need you on the job.'

'Well, they're not going to get me.' He didn't seem particularly interested. 'Go and get dressed, Lesley. I want you to come for a walk with me.'

Lesley didn't stir, apart from tilting her head in order to look up into his face. 'Why?' she asked clearly and suspiciously.

Rad's features tightened as he looked down at the slim sexy body revealed by her minute scarlet bikini.

'My dear Lesley Ann, do you have to sound so distrustful?' he drawled.

She smiled vivaciously. 'You could be planning anything, for all I know, luring me off on my own.'

'By anything, I take you to mean seduction,' Rad mocked. 'If I wanted to make love to you, I would simply pick you up and carry you into the house.'

'To sounds of loud applause from Baptist, I suppose?'

'Undoubtedly. He has his own ideas about the handling of women,' he told her. 'I might try some of them myself if you don't get up off that lounger.'

'You still haven't answered my question,' she reminded him coolly, obeying him only so far as to put her small fine-boned feet on the ground.

A sharp intake of breath warned her of his exasperation. 'All right!' he grated. 'It's cooler in the hills than it is here. I could simply say I'd enjoy your company, but it's not true. I want to talk to you about certain matters pertaining to your father's disappearance.'

It silenced Lesley, and she got up and went into the house without another word. Nervously wondering what might be forthcoming, she changed into jeans and a pink cheesecloth top which hung loosely from a prettily embroidered yoke and buttoned down the front. She added sandals, clipped her shining dark curls back from her face, checked her make-up and went outside again.

The track that they took soon became a narrow path, but after a while they abandoned it and walked along a firebreak. As Rad had said, it was cooler in the hills and the forest on either side of them was a green haven through which a light breeze moved. Ahead of them the mountains rose, dark and immense, some with sheer stone faces, others dark with a tangle of indigenous trees. They forbade approach, chill-looking even in the sunlight, just as they were on the mornings when a lingering mist shrouded them, and Lesley could understand the region's association with the devil's name.

A low rumbling sounded in the distance.

'Thunder,' said Lesley, looking wonderingly at the unbroken blue of the sky.

'Michael doesn't reckon we'll have the storm for a couple of weeks yet.' Rad said dismissively.

'I didn't know one was expected.'

'It's building up. Haven't you noticed how oppressive the atmosphere is?'

'Yes.'

They went on until they found themselves in a dell

through which a tiny silver stream trickled merrily after dropping in a waterfall from a low cliff some distance away. Rad would have gone on, but Lesley stopped him.

'This is nice. I'd like to sit down for a while and you can tell me whatever it is about my father,' she suggested pleasantly.

'Why don't you just say your feet are killing you?' Rad laughed.

'I don't think these sandals were made for walking,' she admitted with a smile.

'But as you say, this is nice,' he relented.

He watched her as she sank to her knees on the soft, short grass and, after a moment, he seated himself on a low, flat rock quite close to her.

Lesley was in profile and the pure, femininely curving line of her throat rose to the firm perfection of her chin, but the features above were revealing a certain amount of unconscious tension at that moment.

'What about my father, Rad?' she asked eventually in a low, strained voice.

Rad bit back a sharp exclamation. 'I had no intention of causing you any apprehension. What I have to say isn't of much importance, nor is it any cause for concern.'

'You relieve me.' Lesley produced a faint, wry smile.

'I've been on the telephone to one or two people in Johannesburg today,' he went on. 'Apparently your own whereabouts have leaked out, as was virtually inevitable, but I don't think, after what I had to say, that we'll have anyone coming up here to bother you. However, I thought I'd better let you know what was said, lest you later accuse me of interfering in your affairs without consulting you.'

'Thank you,' she said tartly. 'However, if you've

effectively prevented any sort of intrusion, I can only be grateful to you. But . . . won't the fraud squad, or whatever, want to interview me?'

'No. One of the people I spoke to was Ewart Brummer, and he assures me that your ignorance of your father's activities has been unconditionally accepted. You couldn't possibly have known. There's only one area in which it's felt you might possibly be of assistance, but you don't have to see anyone; I can relay your answer to the relevant quarters. Lesley, do you have any sort of idea as to your parents' whereabouts?'

'None,' she assured him promptly.

'Think about it,' he advised. 'Did they have any favourite haunts overseas? Places to which they returned quite frequently?'

'One or two,' she recalled after a minute. 'Austria and Switzerland in winter . . . Your story mentioned a Swiss bank account. Monaco and the south of France in summer, and my mother visited Paris quite frequently for clothes. Oh, and they both loved Florida in the States, and California too.'

'No. They're thought to be somewhere in western Europe,' Rad said.

A slightly bitter laugh escaped Lesley. 'Has anyone tried Kandersteg? They and Aunt Thelma and Uncle William could be glaring at each other across the Glühwein at this minute. I'd love to see it.'

'Stop it! Nothing to do with your father really concerns you,' Rad snapped. 'Which is why . . . Well, there was one other thing. I said no, unequivocally, but you'd better confirm it.'

'Yes?' Lesley swallowed nervously.

'The people who are trying to find your father and secure an extradition order were wondering if you would be prepared to assist them in certain ways,' he explained. 'They want you to make some sort of appeal to your parents—they're prepared to fly you out to a major European city from which you can make this appeal, so that your father doesn't feel he's being led into a trap. The Continental papers are running the story and you'd do it through them, I imagine.'

Lesley stared at him. 'I'm not sure if I understand. Am I meant to act as a sort of emotional decoy?'

'Yes.'

Her lips, a dark, dusky pink today, curved into a smile far too cynical in one so young and feminine.

'These people can have no idea of the relationship I had with my parents. If I were dying, they wouldn't respond to an appeal from me,' she informed him.

'I thought as much, so I told them that idea was out,' Rad said quietly.

'You did the right thing—as I'm sure you know.'

'You don't want the chance of seeing them again, hearing their story?' he questioned her.

'No.' Lesley's curls shook as she moved her head from side to side.

'Then put the whole business out of your mind again,' Rad advised.

'I intend to.' Lesley tilted her head to look up at him and her eyes glinted greenly. 'I wouldn't want you to take over my life, Rad Sinclair, but this one aspect of it . . . Well, I'm grateful to you for handling it. So—thank you.'

CHAPTER SIX

LESLEY and Rad were silent for a while, but all about them were the myriad sounds of summer in the Transvaal; the low hum of bees, the shrill urgency of cicadas deep in the forest, the soft slithering of a lizard, other unidentifiable sounds, while closer at hand the little stream gurgled on its way, silvered by the afternoon sun which beat down with an intense heat.

Lesley turned her head and encountered Rad's shadowy grey eyes. She still didn't understand him, she realised with a feeling of frustration. If only she could see into him as she could with others. Why should he be the exception?

Since silence was serving no purpose, she cast about for something to say, remembered her last words to him and suggested lightly, 'You could have said it was a pleasure when I thanked you, Rad.'

'But it wasn't,' he denied blandly.

Lesley smiled. 'I should have guessed. Why do you bother with me, anyway?'

'God knows,' he said disgustedly. 'I suppose because . . . I started this thing.'

'Why did you?'

Rad shrugged impatiently. 'That sort of thing, investigative reporting, isn't my usual line, as you know, and I don't suppose I'll ever do anything like it again. I was supposed to start my leave almost immediately on my return to South Africa, but then I got this line on your father, the merest hint, and I decided I'd like to follow it up myself.'

A sudden thought struck Lesley—suppose it hadn't

been him, but some other journalist? She controlled a shiver and felt glad . . . But she could hardly tell him that.

Instead, she said, 'And you refuse to regard what you've done for me since as . . . as making amends?'

'Don't flatter yourself,' he advised her cruelly. 'I owe you nothing, Lesley, because I did nothing unethical. If you want to feel grateful to someone, there are Mike and Yolande.'

'And deeply grateful to them I am,' Lesley agreed coolly.

'They're more considerate of your feelings than you deserve,' he went on, still on the same hostile note. 'There was something I promised to find out for them.'

'Yes?'

'Dingaan's Day is coming up soon——'

'The Day of the Covenant,' Lesley corrected him mischievously.

'Yes, well!' He laughed and relaxed. 'Like me, they believe that such a solemn commemoration of the battle of Blood River can only create bad feeling between the races, so they treat it as an ordinary holiday. They were contemplating a braai and swimming party, but they're willing to abandon the idea if you feel unable to face a certain amount of inevitable curiosity from their friends when they realise who you are.'

Lesley was touched and remained silent for a few seconds. Then she said softly, 'What kind people your friends are, Rad.'

'Yes . . . Well?'

She searched his face. 'What do you think?'

'I think you'll be all right.'

'Yes.' She inclined her head briefly. 'I'll be all right. After all, I've been accustomed to notoriety.'

'But that earlier notoriety was well deserved,' Rad

murmured sardonically. 'This, however . . . But yes, you'll be able to cope. Just wear your brightest, bravest smile and all the men, at any rate, won't care what your connections are.'

'Shouldn't that read my most seductive smile?' she asked limpidly, and practised just such a smile. 'Will there be lots of men coming?'

'Yes, darling; aren't you pleased?'

'Thrilled.' One of her reckless moods was on her and she continued provocatively, 'As you know, I've learnt something since meeting you. This will be my chance to try out my new knowledge.'

'Say self-knowledge.'

'Then I'd sound like Shanie.'

'All the same, my dear,' Rad continued smoothly, 'I wouldn't attempt to test it just yet. You haven't completed the course yet, remember.'

'One lesson was sufficient,' Lesley responded lightly. 'I'm a quick learner.'

'Nevertheless . . .' He stood up swiftly. 'And while we're on the subject and alone, let's see how much you remember of that first lesson.'

He bent and lifted her to her feet in one swift movement and, unsteady on her feet, Lesley swayed and was caught hard against him. She tilted her head back to find herself looking into his eyes which had darkened almost to blackness.

'This is wholly unnecessary,' she whispered.

'Perhaps it's necessary to me.'

'Yes, well . . .' Lesley paused delicately. 'I suppose you feel obliged to keep your hands off little Shanie when her parents are your friends.'

'Bitch!' he excaimed savagely.

'And there aren't any other young unmarried females about, are there?' Lesley continued daringly, driven by a little devil, wanting to know how far she could go.

'I'm not sure whether I should make love to you or spank you,' he murmured reflectively.

'Would it surprise you very much to know that I would prefer the latter?' Her voice was like a fall of snow, soft and cold and beautiful.

'But how very undignified, Lesley Ann.'

'So is lovemaking, if you think about it.'

'You've a long way to go yet if you think that,' Rad said harshly. 'Allow me to enlighten you.'

He removed the clasps from her hair and threw them away, and then his fingers were entwined in her curls, steadying her head, and he brought his mouth down to meet hers.

Deep in her mind, so deep that she had never consciously admitted it, she had wondered if that weakening warmth, only once experienced, could ever come again. Now she had her answer. It spread through her rapidly, a glow which swiftly became a fire, and she slid her arms round his body under his open shirt and clung to him.

Rad took his mouth away from hers and she cried out, a strange, desolate sound like the cry of a lost angel abandoned by heaven and begging to be taken back.

'Are you learning?' he murmured huskily.

Lesley stared at him wonderingly, then whispered, 'Again,' and turned her lips up to his.

She was all sensation as their mouths became fused once more and she felt his rising hardness against her. Her hands moved feverishly over his smooth back. Then Rad was lowering her to the ground and the sun-warmed grass was soft beneath her as she closed her eyes against the sight of the desire written on his face. His fingers dealt swiftly with the buttons of her loose top and the front fastening of her bra, and when she opened her eyes again it was to see him lowering his head to the firm perfection of her breasts. Shameless cries of delight broke from her lips as his tongue stroked her hardening nipples and she moved her hands until they were touching his head, stroking the dark hair.

'Rad . . . oh, Rad, please!'

She didn't know what she was pleading for. She only knew that she was being drawn inexorably closer and closer to the brink of something she couldn't begin to comprehend. Passion racked her body, a passion dark and vibrant and exciting, and she made no move to stop him when he undid the zip of her jeans. His hands were warm and hard on her body, caressing her flat stomach and hips, and moving up again over her rib-cage to her breasts and shoulders, stroking, awakening, rousing her, until her hips moved sensuously.

Only then did Rad lower himself on to her, his weight a sweet heaviness, and Lesley writhed erotically beneath him, her breasts crushed against his hard chest, while their mouths locked in another kiss of unbounded desire. He raised his head and she looked up into his face, seeing the perspiration beading his brow, and seeing the passion darkening his eyes.

'I want you, Lesley.' His voice was a hoarse gasp. 'I want you here and now!'

For a moment she pressed her mouth to the wound on his left shoulder, but his words had recalled her sanity and an instant later she was striving to be free, pushing at him with a strength born of fear.

'No!'

Rad rolled away from her and sat up. 'What is it?'

'I can't,' Lesley murmured.

His eyes were still smouldering with desire, but his mouth tightened at her words.

'What's wrong?' he demanded harshly.

Still shaken by the storm he had created within her, Lesley shook her head, and he made an impatient movement towards her.

'Nothing?' he challenged, his hand going to the belt of his jeans. 'So why the interruption?'

'Because——' Lesley sat up abruptly. 'You're never going to believe this, Rad.'

'What now?' he asked with mounting anger.

Lesley hesitated, her swollen lips moving soundlessly as she strove for some small measure of self-control. Finally she managed a wan smile.

'I'm a virgin,' she confessed clearly.

'Joke of the year,' Rad snapped. 'This isn't a game, Lesley Ann. I want you.'

'I knew you wouldn't believe me.' She refastened her bra. 'But it's true.'

'For pity's sake!' he exclaimed furiously. 'If you don't want to go any further, why not simply say so instead of inventing an excuse . . . the most ludicrous lie I've ever heard!'

'All right! I don't want to take this any further,' she said vehemently, and her eyes flashed a brilliant green. 'But the other thing happens to be true too. I am a virgin.'

'Get your clothes fixed up,' he advised coldly, standing up and moving back to the rock on which he had sat earlier.

Lesley zipped up her jeans and buttoned her shirt with fingers that shook a little. How could she convince him of the truth? Why bother, anyway? Yet now, suddenly and desperately, she wanted him to believe it. Unable to find the clips he had discarded, she stood up and walked slowly towards him.

'I don't believe you,' he told her flatly.

'Why would I lie?'

'That's what I'm wondering,' he said in a chilling voice. 'I can think of several reasons, none very pleasant.'

'The fact is that I've told you the truth.' Lesley tried a smile. 'I know it seems incredible.'

'And that's an understatement!'

'Please believe me.'

'How can I?' Rad had seated himself on the rock and Lesley knelt in front of him once more. 'The only way I can ever find out the truth is by possessing you.'

'And . . . and I don't want that.'

'Why not?' he asked unexpectedly.

'You're . . . you're a stranger, virtually,' she faltered. 'I . . . I hardly know you.'

'So what? Oh, but I'm already forgetting,' he derided. 'You're a virgin.'

The way he spat that last word made Lesley flinch, but she held his gaze.

'Yes. I apologise for misleading you before,' she said quietly.

'I think you're misleading me now,' he contradicted her roughly. 'Or attempting to. I remain unconvinced by this sudden protestation of innocence. After all, darling, I've heard some of your ex-lovers on the subject of sweet Lesley Ann.'

'They were all lying,' she said icily. 'May I explain?'

'Please do,' Rad invited her urbanely. 'And while you're about it, you might also explain just why, if this virginity line is the truth, you chose to let everyone believe a lie?'

'I'll try, but it's difficult to do,' she said.

'I'll bet,' he agreed sardonically. 'But proceed, my dear. You've at least got off to a good start by managing to sound relatively sincere.'

'Please.' She put out a hand to touch his knee briefly. 'Listen to me. If you don't believe me, I won't blame you, but listen first and then judge. I have this gift, though it often seems more like a curse, of being able to see through the facades people erect. If I didn't have it, I would probably have fallen in love with someone long ago and believed he loved me in return. As it is, I've been able to sense that every man I've been out with since I was sixteen has cared nothing about me, though they've all pretended to. Once I tried to make myself ugly, but I couldn't change my body, so now I make myself beautiful, and devastate them. I can see how sceptical you're looking, Rad . . . but with your experience you must have discovered that women want emotion as well as the physical act of lovemaking. I found it offensive that they only wanted my body, so . . . well, I took revenge on all of them. I would lead them on and then say, "No, I'm sorry" . . . And this is where I would feel superior, because every last one of them would believe that the fault lay with him. They couldn't believe that Lesley Ann Crosnier had never responded to any man, and I never enlightened them. They were all very young men, of course, nicely brought up young men who would never dream of using force . . . I doubt if an older man would have reacted in the same way.'

'You're right there,' Rad inserted tauntingly. 'You deserve to roast for what you did to those poor young fools—if what you say is true, which I still doubt. They've probably all got hang-ups for life, each thinking he's been rejected by Lesley Ann Crosnier when all about him others have received her favours . . . Presumably that's what they all thought?'

'Yes.' Even now Lesley couldn't contain a small, malicious smile. 'Each thought he was the only one . . . and couldn't face admitting it in those disgustingly cynical male gatherings when everyone discusses his conquests. I don't know when or with whom it began, but someone told the first lie, and so I got my reputation.'

'You little bitch,' he condemned her disgustedly. 'How you manipulated those poor young devils!'

Lesley raised her chin in a gesture of pride. 'Try looking at it from my point of view: how they insulted me by wanting to use my body while caring nothing for me.'

'Why should they care?' he taunted contemptuously. 'I may have roused your body to awareness, but the rest of you remains cold and uncaring. You're still emotionally frigid.'

She bowed her head again. 'There's no answer to that, is there?' she conceded in a small, carefully controlled voice. 'I haven't loved anyone since my granny, and I've only liked a few . . . Chrissie, Heather Louw and now Yolande and Michael. I know I'm flawed, Rad, but I don't know why and there's nothing I can do about it. I can't love when I can see so clearly the small-minded selfishness of people.'

'I imagine your parents have a lot to answer for,' Rad said abruptly as he stood up. Lesley remained kneeling on the grass and he looked down at her broodingly. 'And may I ask why I have been privileged with what you claim to be the truth?'

The question disconcerted her, and she gulped. 'You're . . . different,' she faltered, and he smiled sardonically. 'You . . . you're older, and you were the only one to realise at once that I wasn't responding to you. And then later you made me . . . feel something.'

'And so?' he probed relentlessly.

'And so . . . nothing!' Lesley stood up. 'You surely understand that as I possess no sexual experience, I don't feel ready to make love with . . . just anyone.'

'I'm not just anyone, Lesley,' Rad grated. 'I'm the man who's enabled you to experience physical pleasure, as you yourself have admitted, and I could give you even greater pleasure.'

'I'm not ready,' she repeated calmly.

'Will you ever be?'

'I don't know.' Having got her confession over with, she could feel her composure flowing back into her and she was able to give him an appealing smile. 'I have to ask—do you believe what I've told you?'

'I'm not sure.' Rad studied her face reflectively. 'You're obviously aware of how incredible your story appears. It hardly seems possible that at twenty and a virgin you could have carried out such a gigantic hoax against the males in your circle without being found out . . . On the other hand, you're an exceptional young woman in many ways and an excellent actress, so I suppose it just might be the truth that you've told me. I'll need to think about it.'

'Let me know what decision you reach,' she invited coolly.

'I will. You can be very sure of that,' he replied, and Lesley thought she detected a threatening note in his voice. 'Shall we walk back to the farm now?'

'Definitely.' Lesley was malicious. 'I can just picture Shanie's disappointment if she gets back from town and you're not there to admire her new hairstyle. The New Shanie Ward, with her personality emerging.'

'Poor Shanie,' Rad laughed as they left behind them the little dell where Lesley had been so shattered by the force of the storm he had summoned up within her body. She knew she would never forget it.

'Shanie doesn't need sympathy,' she said.

'Why do you dislike her?'

'I've looked into her mind,' Lesley informed him coldly.

'Ah, yes, this gift you have,' Rad murmured.

'I suppose you disbelieve that as well?' she challenged, just slightly ill at ease because it was an unusual ability that she possessed and very few people had been told of it.

'On the contrary,' Rad denied smoothly. 'I've suspected something a little more than mere intelligence since the first time we met, when you made such an accurate diagnosis of Heather Louw's worth . . . But tell me, Lesley, have you taken a look at me in that way?'

'That's what's so frustrating,' she told him with a confiding little smile. 'I've tried and tried, but I just can't seem to see you. You're hidden from me, and that's never happened before. I told Heather and she figured it was because you're on a different plane.'

Rad's smile contained a wealth of cruel mockery. 'Poor Lesley Ann! So you'll never know just why I want you.'

'No. That's why you'll never have me,' she returned evenly.

'I wouldn't be so sure of that, darling,' Rad warned her, and Lesley shivered at the steely resolve in his voice.

Lesley was acutely conscious of being under observation in the days following her confession to Rad. He was watching her, she knew, speculating about her, torturing her by taking his time before letting her know whether he believed what she had told him or not.

Frequently she would feel herself being watched and look up to find his eyes on her, cool, smoke-grey eyes which were never anything but inscrutable save when occasionally they were derisive. She would meet his regard as coolly as she knew how, with one of her most beautiful smiles, but she was aware of a rare tension building up inside her.

Shanie, too, had noticed that Rad watched Lesley a lot, and put her own construction on the fact.

'Rad is forever watching you,' she commented one

evening, having entered Lesley's room to see what she could borrow.

'Perhaps he doesn't trust me,' Lesley suggested lightly without looking up from her task of painting her nails.

'No, no,' Shanie laughed. 'Not in that way.'

'In what way, then?' Lesley was amused.

Shanie sounded young and sad. 'I suppose it was inevitable. I knew I hadn't a chance, but I did so hope . . . Oh, Lesley, he must be falling in love with you.'

'There's a one-word answer to that, but I won't say it.'

Shanie gave her one of her delightfully vague looks. 'What? Oh, just think of the responsibility if Rad was . . . interested in you. He would demand so much, but it would be such a privilege to contribute to his happiness.' She paused breathlessly, gasped, and, when she resumed, did so in a tone of horror. 'Oh, Lesley, when you suggested you'd take revenge for his exposing your father . . . You were only joking, weren't you?'

'Nonsense. I was voicing my most earnest intention,' Lesley insisted humorously. Shanie often irritated her, but she was in the mood to play up to her at this moment.

'Oh, but . . .' Shanie's voice died away.

'Yes?' Lesley prompted, her sensitive mind aware of Shanie's as the girl wondered how to play this.

'No! No!' Shanie had decided, and was shaking her head with a guilelessly trusting smile transforming her face. 'I just know you're joking. I believe in you.'

'And the intrinsic goodness of my heart.'

'Don't laugh at me, Lesley,' Shanie begged. 'I know you want me to think you're hard and cruel, but I'm convinced that basically you're not like that at all.'

Sweet words, but false, for Lesley had no difficulty, now or ever, in perceiving the currents of dislike which ran from Shanie to her. The girl had never liked her, but since she refrained from overt hostility, Lesley felt little fear of her. Shanie couldn't harm her . . .

Dingaan's Day arrived and Lesley's nerves still jangled whenever she knew Rad was watching her. The day before, she had helped Yolande with preparations for the party, and that morning she assisted her with the salads.

'You've done enough, Lesley,' Yolande said eventually. 'Now go and put on something really stunning. People will start arriving soon, including a number of young men whom I'd be glad to see taking an interest in Shanie . . . If she sees them taking an interest in you instead, it might finally get home to her that the little-girl-lost approach is better discarded.'

Reluctantly Lesley went up to her room and changed into a short, cool wrap-around skirt which emphasised the slenderness of her waist while its dead-whiteness enhanced the soft tan the afternoons beside the pool had given her legs. With it she teamed a tight red cotton-knit top, simple but sexy since it was sleeveless and plunged sharply in front. Already a few guests had arrived, she realised, as she did her hair in a sophisticated style, drawn severely back from her face with just a few curling tendrils allowed to soften the effect. She checked her make-up for the second time, deliberately delaying, put on perfume, changed her gold earrings for silver ones, tried on various silver bangles and rings . . .

'Fool,' she said to her flawless reflection in the mirror.

Foolish it might be, but for once in her life Lesley was unable to conquer a certain nervousness. From outside came the sound of many voices—too many. They would be curious about her; people would stare when they discovered her identity. As Yolande had said, several young men would be present and they would flock around her as they always did, but with Rad watching her, judging her, how was she to achieve the composure she required for the battery of smiles, the sweep of fluttering eyelashes which were part of the social game she played?

And why should she care about him anyway?

Her hands shook as she removed a ring from her middle finger.

There was a knock at the door and it flew open. She spun round on the stool to stare at Rad, casually dressed in jeans and a soft blue-and-grey shirt.

'Still titivating?' he enquired with mild exasperation. 'Yolande was wondering what had become of you.'

Lesley stood up slowly, trying to take deep calming breaths, but, ridiculously, her heart was palpitating and her pulses fluttering.

'I was ready long ago,' she said as coolly as she could.

'Then why are you still hanging around up here?' he demanded impatiently.

Her curving red mouth smiled but her shadowy-green eyes were frightened. 'I was hiding,' she confessed a trifle bitterly.

He searched her face. 'From whom? All those people out there?'

'No, from you!' Lesley laughed shakily. 'Oh, damn you, Rad Sinclair! You watch me and watch me, and I can't take any more. I can't face all those people and their inevitable curiosity and perhaps distrust . . . not with you looking on all the time, condemning me. I can't stand it.'

'Stage-fright,' he laughed. 'I didn't think you possessed any nerves.'

'Well, I do, and you're aggravating them by your attitude,' she said plaintively. 'I'm not going outside.'

His hands grasped her shoulders and something like an electric shock ran through her as he shook her.

'Listen to me, Lesley Ann Crosnier.' His voice was compelling, and she felt she could believe anything he said. 'You are going to go outside and I will be beside you. If I watch you, it will be with admiration for the way you're handling yourself in a difficult situation. You're going to captivate them all with your most bewitching smile. They'll know who you are, but you're equal to them because you have nothing to be ashamed of. So—no humility.'

She lifted her chin. 'No humility,' she repeated. 'Do I look all right?'

Rad appraised her critically. 'Perhaps a little more colour on your cheeks. You're a bit pale.' He smiled. 'Otherwise you're perfect, as you well know, you young witch. You ought to wear your hair like that more often. Your cheekbones are wonderful.'

'Thank you.' She smiled as she applied a little more blusher. His praise had restored her confidence and she knew that everything would be as he had said. He would not watch her critically today, and she would make the strangers outside forget that she was Gerard Crosnier's daughter.

Rad was strength, someone to lean on—figuratively. As they went outside together and she felt herself the cynosure of all eyes, Lesley would have liked to slip her hand into his, but that, she realised sadly, would be going too far. Then he would return to mocking. She must stand alone, but she would still experience the support he was giving her, moral support, and that must satisfy her.

He evidently knew most of the Wards' friends from his previous visits to the farm, and he didn't leave her, but took her around and introduced her to everyone. There was, as she had expected, curiosity in the looks they gave her, but these people were tactful and friendly and she soon sensed their admiration, especially the men's, and knew that she had conquered.

Only once did her extra sense perceive a wave of antipathy directed at her, and that came from Shanie. She looked at the girl, but no trace of her feelings was visible in Shanie's sweetly smiling face. She was dressed all in white, in a full-skirted dress with a thin strip of lace round the neckline. Her fair hair remained long after her visit to the hairdresser, but it had been trimmed round the ends and now curled under. Today she wore it up in two bunches tied with white ribbons and Lesley thought she looked sweet—but more like a child at her first Communion than a young adult at an adult party.

Rad brought her a drink and stayed with her for a little longer, but by now some of the young men to whom she had been introduced were beginning to drift into her orbit, and eventually he smiled at her.

'You'll be all right now, won't you?'

'I'm in my element,' she assured him with a radiant smile.

'I can see that. You're doing very well.'

But as he moved away to join Michael at the braai, Lesley watched him go with regret. These young men were nice enough, but callow in comparison to Rad, and she would rather have had him at her side than a dozen of these others who now flocked round her.

As swiftly as the thought had come, she dismissed it and devoted herself to working her magic. This was a party, that social activity she enjoyed above all others, and no time for introspection.

After the braaied lunch, some of the young males invaded the pool, but those with more consideration for their digestions waited a while. When Lesley finally appeared in her scarlet bikini, her success was reaffirmed and she sat on the edge of the pool, dangling her slim legs in the water, with a cluster of young men about her.

The party went on all day and her conquests continued effortlessly, but for once her heart wasn't wholly in the game. She didn't want to make fools of these young men—or any young men, any more.

When one of them suggested a walk, just the two of them, late in the afternoon, she refused as kindly as she could, and tried to tactfully discourage him when he promised that he would be telephoning her soon.

Her long, slanting eyes were wistful as she glanced towards Rad who, with Shanie and another equally pretty but older girl, was relaxing on the emerald green lawn beyond the pool area. He was laughing gently at something Shanie was saying, laughing in that indulgent way he reserved exclusively for her, but then he looked up and caught sight of Lesley. The laughter died instantly from his face; instead he looked displeased and raised his eyebrows interrogatively.

Lesley felt a little as if he had caught her spying on him, but she pouted naughtily, shaking her head, before swinging round and moving gracefully away.

A short while later he came to her where she stood beside the pool. She was wearing her white skirt and scarlet top again by this time, and her small feet were in scarlet high-heeled sandals which matched her toenails. She was standing alone, watching a few of the most energetic of "her" young men who were showing off in the water—for her benefit, as she realised with a faint feeling of amusement.

'Is something wrong?' Rad asked, standing beside her.

Lesley turned her small perfectly shaped head slowly and gave him her most brilliant smile. 'What could possibly be wrong?' She permitted her glance to stray to the young men in the pool.

'Lesley Ann rides again,' Rad taunted sardonically, following her gaze. 'A triumph, one might call it. They came, they saw, they fell. Tell me, which one have you selected to be the next victim of your eternal revenge on the male sex?'

Lesley's long curling lashes swept down over her eyes and then fluttered up again. 'Would you believe, darling, none of them?' she said demurely. 'One asked me to go for a lonely walk with him just now—that fair one doing the belly-flop—and I refused him. I did it quite nicely too.'

'Can it be that you've reformed . . . undergone a change of heart?' Rad queried on a falsely dramatic note.

'Can it be?' she repeated flippantly. 'I don't know. I only know that . . . I'd like my Duiwelskloof reputation to be different from the one I have in Johannesburg.'

'Or can it be that now you've learnt to respond to a man's lovemaking you're afraid of letting yourself go and losing the virginity you claim still to have?' he challenged with deliberate cruelty.

Lesley refused to drop her gaze. 'You don't really believe that,' she said softly. 'You know you're the only one who can make me . . . feel like that.'

'Should I be flattered?' he drawled.

'No. I attribute the fact solely to your maturity and experience, nothing else,' she told him with gentle malice. 'But please tell me: have you concluded that I was telling the truth about myself the other day?'

'Is it important to you?'

Lesley considered, schooling her features into a smooth, smiling mask. 'Only in the sense that, like everyone else, I'd like to be believed when I tell the truth. What have you decided, Rad?'

'I honestly don't know,' he replied slowly. 'You've

lied and misled and deceived so much in the past, haven't you? I suppose I'll never know until I've had you.'

'Which you never will,' she promised quietly.

And far away, beyond the mountains, thunder growled ominously.

CHAPTER SEVEN

Now began Lesley's obsession. Rad Sinclair had become an object of intense fascination for her. Where he was likely to be found, there she was, never obtrusive or importunate, but always fascinated by something about him, something she was forever on the verge of comprehending yet never quite managed to grasp. At night, as she slid down into sleep, some facial expression or something he had said that day would suddenly return to jolt her into wakefulness and she would lie awake, endeavouring to fathom the man who was such an enigma.

She recognised her obsession as such and acknowledged the folly of it, yet was powerless to combat it.

If only something would happen, she thought a thousand times. If only there were some challenge she could issue . . .

Three days after the Dingaan's Day braai, she found herself bored. She had only seen Rad at breakfast which they all ate outside these hot days, and he had seemed abstracted, unable even to cast her a mocking smile when Yolande had teased her about the fact that the telephone had been ringing ever since the party and that Lesley had refused all invitations to go out. In fact, the only outing she had had was yesterday's when she had accompanied Rad and Michael to the not far distant country club for a short time.

He had disappeared immediately the meal was over, so she had ridden alone with Shanie and returned to hear the sound of a typewriter being used in the rondawel cottage. She had shrugged discontentedly. Usually he only worked in the afternoons.

When, after lunch, the staccato sound, interspersed with frequent pauses of varying length, continued to issue from the rondawel cottage, she made up her mind.

Shanie was already in the swimming pool and Lesley had been going to join her presently, but now she abandoned the idea of exchanging her denim shorts and pale apple-green top for a bikini, and set off in the direction of the cottage. She was in the shade of the oak tree when the sound of typing ceased. The door to the central rectangular room stood open and she approached it curiously, having never previously seen inside.

Rad, shirtless and barefooted, wearing only jeans, had his back to her. He was seated at the large imbuia desk against the window opposite the door with the typewriter in front of him and an untidy pile of typescript pushed to one side. Files and newspaper cuttings littered the rest of the desk, with an untouched cup of coffee balanced precariously on one corner. Rad wasn't typing at that moment and Lesley saw that he was smoking, something she had never seen him do before. As she watched, however, he gave an exclamation of disgust and stubbed the cigarette out in a copper ashtray which already contained several butts. She saw his right hand move up to his left shoulder and massage it absently, as if the partially healed muscles were aching.

'Rad.'

He didn't turn his head. 'What do you want, Lesley?' he asked sharply.

'To see you. May I come in?' she requested politely.

'No.' Just that one word.

'Rad . . .' Lesley took a step into the room which

had attractive Persian rugs scattered about the floor but was otherwise the untidiest room she had seen.

'Get out of here,' he ordered harshly.

'Why?' she challenged provocatively. 'Haven't you worked long enough for one day? You're supposed to be on leave, sick leave, I think, and I can see your shoulder is worrying you.'

'Don't tell me you came here out of solicitude for my health,' he taunted her, at last turning his head, and she was shocked by the fatigue which had become etched into his face since that morning.

'All right, I came for purely selfish reasons,' she admitted with an appealing smile. 'I wanted to ask you something.'

'It will have to wait,' he said shortly.

'Rad, please, it's important.'

'Get the hell out of here!' he shouted. 'Go on—I'm busy. I don't want to see you or hear you, so scram!'

Already he was turning back to the typewriter, and Lesley shrugged defeatedly. 'We learn something every day,' she commented resignedly. 'I didn't know you could lose your temper like that. All right, don't throw anything—I'm going.'

She went outside and sat down on the wooden bench which always stood under the oak tree. All about her the garden was a blaze of colour, but she saw none of it. She heard him start typing again, swear violently and then stop. A moment later he appeared at the door.

'Fetch me a beer from the house,' he instructed her.

Lesley smiled ruefully and stood up. No please, no apology for his rudeness, but she was glad enough to obey him.

When she returned with a couple of icy-cold cans, he was standing at the window looking out over the citrus groves below.

'Thanks.' He took the cans from her. 'Want one?'

'I don't like beer.'

He pulled the ring tab off one. 'I'm sorry I yelled at you just now, Lesley,' he said easily.

'That's all right. I shouldn't have disturbed you. Is something going badly—or so well that you can't bear interruption?'

'Badly.' He smiled tiredly and indicated the pile of typescript. 'It's a commissioned book on the recurring revolutionary theme in Africa, but I find it difficult to be objective about some of the things I've witnessed.'

'I can understand that.' She studied his face critically. 'Take a break, why don't you?'

'This beer and the sight of your legs are all I need,' he mocked.

'I'm glad to be of assistance in your recovery,' she told him flippantly. 'May I have a look round?'

'Please do. I'll sit here and enjoy the view,' he drawled, his eyes travelling up from her smooth tanned legs, over her hips and waist to the low rounded neckline of her clinging top.

Lesley ignored him and began a short tour of inspection. At one end of the central room with its chairs and low striped couch, a rondawel had been turned into a large kitchen. The half-sized fridge was switched on, but contained nothing but a bottle of water and a tray of ice, and apart from that there was nothing to see but coffee-making equipment and a jar of coffee beans. She recrossed the centre room. The door to the other rondawel was closed, but Rad inclined his head when she indicated her wish to open it. This one was divided into a small bathroom and fair-sized bedroom. The latter contained a double bed, and Lesley recalled what Shanie had once said about the women who sometimes came here with him.

'Does anyone else use this cottage?' she asked, leaving the door ajar and returning to him in the centre room.

'No. It's mine.'

'And everything in it?' She glanced at the low bookshelves running along one wall, wondering if his choice of reading matter might tell her anything about him.

'Yes.'

'Do you have a home in Johannesburg?'

'A furnished flat which I sublet while I'm away.' He grimaced. 'I usually return to Johannesburg without any warning and consequently have to use a hotel.'

Lesley knelt on a glowing Persian rug and looked at the titles in the bookshelf, but they told her nothing except that he liked both fiction and non-fiction. Sartre and Kafka were wedged next to John Wyndham's S.F. books, Solzhenitsyn was flanked by Hermann Hesse's *Siddhartha* and Richard Adams' *Shardik*.

She rose and went to sit down on the couch. Rad was sprawled in a low chair opposite her and to her right was a music centre and a stack of records and tapes. These offered no clue either. Heavy rock, classics and film soundtracks were interspersed with other genres, and Lesley gave it up.

She found Rad watching her with a certain amount of amusement. 'What are you looking for?' he asked idly.

'A clue,' she said with a theatrical gesture.

'Ah, yes. I'm obscured from your exceptional vision for some reason,' he murmured reflectively. 'You'll never know me, Lesley.'

'That's what I'm afraid of.'

'We might, of course, know each other in the biblical sense,' he suggested with faint menace.

'Not just now, thank you, darling,' she retorted flippantly. 'I've other things on my mind.'

'Such as?' He set his beer can down on the floor

beside his chair. 'Why did you come looking for me, Lesley?'

Lesley hesitated. 'Second thoughts are perhaps wiser,' she said finally, and digressed rapidly, 'I didn't know you smoked.'

'A bad habit I've been able to give up except when I've a typewriter in front of me,' Rad volunteered indifferently. His eyes narrowed. 'Out with it, Lesley. What did you want?'

She sighed. 'I should never have allowed you to persuade me to leave Johannesburg, Rad.'

'Why? What's gone wrong?' he asked abruptly.

'Nothing new,' she assured him carefully, spreading her hands and looking at her long nails which were, as always, flawless. She looked up again and realised that he was waiting for her to continue. 'What am I doing here, going out horse-riding every morning and swimming and sunbathing every afternoon? I'm not achieving anything. I should have remained in Johannesburg and started looking for employment immediately.'

'As you yourself have said, what sort of job could you get without qualifications?' Rad prompted her evenly.

'I don't know.' Lesley shrugged. 'Perhaps I could work on the make-up counter in one of the big shops. They like their assistants to be . . . good-looking, and I'd quite enjoy it.'

'For a time; then you'd find yourself bored.'

'You're not very encouraging, are you?' Lesley challenged accusingly. 'I can't continue like this indefinitely. Eventually I'll have to settle for something like that. My more immediate worry, however, is . . . Rad, I'm embarrassed financially. It's—what?—six days until Christmas and the few rand I've got in my purse will barely cover the cost of shampoo and a few other things I've run out of. I'm not going to be able to give the Wards presents, which I would have liked to do . . . I know they'll understand, but I shall nevertheless be mortified.'

'Oh, hell!' Rad exclaimed disgustedly, sitting up straight. 'I thought of that some time ago and then forgot to mention it to you. I'll take you into Tzaneen tomorrow and cash a cheque for you. You'll be able to buy your presents then.'

Lesley felt at a loss. 'I can't accept your money, Rad,' she said quietly.

'Why not?' His eyes glinted coldly. 'A loan if you like, Lesley. You can pay me back one day.'

'But——'

'Don't make a song and dance about it,' he snapped. 'It's the obvious solution, isn't it, especially as I'm in a way responsible for the situation you're in.'

She sensed that he would grow even more impatient if she protested further. 'Oh, well, all right,' she gave in reluctantly. 'But it means that the Wards' presents from me will be paid for with your money.'

'I know it's far from ideal,' he conceded, relaxing again. 'But it's the best we can do under the circumstances—Unless you'd care to sell your story to a newspaper? Perhaps one of the Sundays? They'd pay well.'

Lesley paled beneath her make-up. 'No!' she exclaimed sharply. Then, distrustfully, 'You weren't serious, were you?'

'Perhaps I was testing you,' he drawled.

'I'll accept a loan from you and pay you back at the first possible moment,' she said coldly.

'There's no hurry.'

Suddenly she gave him a melting smile. 'You needn't worry that you'll be paying for your own present. I've got that already.'

'Now I'm intrigued.' He eyed her speculatively.

'I don't know if you'll like it, but at least it will amuse you,' she continued, with delicious anticipation adding charm to her slow-spoken, clear words.

'If it's amusing, at least it can't be lethal,' Rad retorted. 'All the same, Lesley, I sense mischief.'

'No, no, it's nothing . . . nasty,' she assured him. 'It's just funny. You'll laugh at me, I know, but I'm still determined to give it to you.'

'I can hardly wait,' he taunted. 'Anyway, that's settled. I'll take you down to Tzaneen immediately after breakfast tomorrow. Ask Shanie if she'd like to come with us.'

'She'll come,' Lesley predicted. 'Thank you, Rad. All the same, I'd better start giving some thought to my future. It's obvious that I won't be able to return to Varsity in February.'

'You'll get your degree,' Rad predicted confidently.

'How can I?' she questioned sadly.

'Stop worrying about it,' he advised. 'Just believe what I say.'

'I can't,' Lesley demurred. Little sparks of resentment made her eyes a purer green than usual. 'Do you know how many thousands of people do B.A.s? I'll never get a bursary.'

'And judging by your initial reaction to my offer of a small loan, you'll never allow me to pay for the completion of your course,' he said expressionlessly.

'You're dead right,' Lesley confirmed, concealing her shock. 'How can you even think of such a thing?'

'Easily.' His smile mocked her. 'We'll have to think of some alternative solution—or I will. I don't want you worrying about this, so put it out of your mind.'

'That's a tall order.'

'It wouldn't be, if you'd just have a little faith.'

'In you?' Lesley enquired sceptically.

'Why not?'

And indeed, why not? she thought. Nothing daunted Rad. If he set out to achieve something, achieve it he would. If he said she would get her degree, then that was what she must believe.

'I wish I understood you,' she said in a shivery little voice.

Rad's answering smile was strange. 'Perhaps you will one day,' he suggested as she stood up and stretched. 'But give it up to today, darling. I'd like to get back to work.'

Lesley remained where she was, crossing her slim legs and draping one slender arm along the back of the couch.

'Meaning that I'm to remove myself from your presence?'

'Precisely.' His eyes glittered, but he didn't smile. 'If you were to stay, even if I kept my back to you, I'd be aware of you sitting there . . . Those legs, Lesley Ann, are fatal.'

'So I've been told on a number of occasions,' she agreed with cool complacency, smiling up into his eyes with deadly enticement.

'Are you trying to provoke me?' Rad muttered furiously, taking a step towards her. 'You're playing a dangerous game, my dear, because you can't be sure just which particular fate you'll be calling down on yourself.'

She arched her dark, beautifully shaped eyebrows in delicate amusement. 'Perhaps the spanking . . . this time?' she murmured.

'Kinky,' Rad drawled. His eyes flashed sudden fire. 'Get out of here, Lesley.'

'I find Shanie's company just a little tedious at times.' Her red lips pouted provocatively. 'You brought me up here, Rad. Shouldn't you make an effort to entertain me occasionally?'

'All right!' he agreed explosively. 'How would you like to be entertained?'

'We could go on talking?'

'We've talked enough,' Rad said tightly. 'I'll entertain you, sweetheart, but I'll choose the method.'

He was moving towards her with the silent ease of a jungle cat and Lesley felt her heart constrict painfully, but she managed to go on smiling.

'I think I've changed my mind, Rad,' she said—just a trifle breathlessly—and uncrossed her legs, preparing to stand up.

'It's too late, Lesley,' he countered, and his face was cold and dangerous. 'Way, way too late.'

He jerked her roughly to her feet and slid his arms round her body, tightening them until she had no hope of escaping him.

'This wasn't what I meant,' she protested faintly, looking up into contemptuous grey eyes.

'Don't lie to me yet again,' he taunted, his lips very close to hers. 'You knew what you were inviting. Very well, my dear, you shall have it. We'll entertain each other and exchange regrets and recriminations afterwards.'

A wild, reckless excitement tore at Lesley as she understood the import of his words. She lifted her hands to his chest, not to push him away, but to caress, with sweeping circular movements, the hard flesh, the tangle of fine dark hairs tickling her palms.

'Lesley!' Rad groaned her name, his anger evaporating as his own desire flared.

Her lips were parted in eager invitation even before his had touched them, and when he did finally claim her mouth, she swayed against him.

The door was open, but not a breath of wind stirred

the torrid afternoon, and its heat seemed transferred to their bloodstreams as they stood locked together, their mouths a single unit giving expression to the swirling desire that invaded their bodies. It was a kiss that seemed endless, a violent, hungry taking and giving. Lesley shuddered convulsively and clung more feverishly to Rad, sure that she must die in this terrible, wonderful storm that shook through her, causing her hips to rotate erotically against the hardness of his body.

But now at last Rad was picking her up, carrying her into his bedroom and laying her down on the double bed. He undressed her with swift violence, exploring and caressing every inch of her heated body until she cried his name.

'Rad! Rad!' She didn't recognise her own voice, so strange and wild did it sound in this moment of abandoned desire.

'Oh, God, you're so beautiful,' he groaned deeply, touching her turgid breasts with hard fingers, his breathing rapid.

He left the bed to remove his jeans and Lesley lay where she was, trembling with an excitement she couldn't control, her passion-glazed eyes a dark, brilliant green as they caressed his magnificent body.

She gave a glad little gasp as he flung himself down on her and devoured her mouth with his again. Her body writhed sensuously beneath his, then arched rigidly as she felt the intimate pressure of his thighs between her legs.

'I want you, I want you,' he told her achingly.

'Hurry,' she moaned yearningly. 'Oh, Rad, I can't wait. Love me, quickly!'

But instead of taking full possession of her, he rolled off her and lay on his side, his smouldering smoke-coloured eyes searching her flushed face.

'God, Lesley Ann!' he ground out savagely. 'Do you know what you're doing to me? Look at me, feel me! I'm still in control now, but only just, believe me.'

'You don't have to be. I'm not frightened,' she whispered, drawing him to her like the Lorelei, eyes witch-green, glowing with the mysterious power of her femininity.

'No!' He flung away from her. His face was taut, his voice intense. 'You've claimed to be a virgin, which I still can't believe. If you want to keep that questionable purity, get dressed now.'

'But why?' She trailed shaking fingers over his damp skin. 'Take me, Rad.'

'Now? Here, like this? With the cottage door open and Shanie or someone liable to walk in at any moment?' he derided.

Lesley snatched her hand away from him. 'I'd forgotten Shanie,' she admitted bleakly. Her unfulfilled longing was torment, but she managed a valiant little smile. 'Perhaps she has exclusive rights to this bed. Tell me, Rad, when Shanie forgets her pride and begs to be made love to, do you humiliate her as you've just humiliated me?'

'Shanie doesn't tempt me as you've been doing ever since we met,' he responded harshly, sitting up and reaching for his jeans. 'You may or may not be a virgin, Lesley, I don't know, but you've the soul of a tart. You're forever flaunting yourself . . . Oh, God!'

He gave it up and put on his jeans, standing beside the bed and looking down on the nakedness of her beautiful body with the lingering traces of his passion still kindling his eyes.

'I hate you,' Lesley informed him cordially, lifting her suddenly aching body from the bed and looking for her clothes.

'Why?' Rad's voice was silkily unpleasant. 'What

have I done to you that you haven't done to a dozen or more men?—if your story is true. You lead them on and then deny them, didn't you say?'

'I never lead them on that far, but I guess I deserved that,' she conceded huskily. 'All the same, Rad, I'll never forgive you. This is the first time I've ever offered myself to anyone like that and you . . . you rejected me. I could be scarred for life by that.'

Rad laughed. 'You're very funny at times. I haven't rejected you, sweetheart; I've merely postponed the hour of our mutual enjoyment. This afternoon was inconvenient. I promise you that one day soon I'll make love to you fully, Lesley.'

'Sorry,' she said casually, wriggling into her shorts. 'The offer is now closed—and it won't be repeated. From now on, I'm exclusive.'

His eyes narrowed. 'When I decide to make love to you, there'll be nothing you can do about it.'

'Oh, yes, there will.' She pulled on her pale green top and tucked it into her shorts. 'It will be my turn to do the rejecting then, Rad. I'll make you pay for what you've done to me today.'

'How very melodramatic!' His smile was infinitely arrogant. 'You want me quite as much as I want you, darling. If I touch you, I don't think you'll be in any state to reject me.'

'Shall we lay bets on it?' Lesley enquired pleasantly, finding a mirror and running her fingers through her curls.

'It's hardly worth the trouble, my dear.'

'You disappoint me.' She turned from the mirror and faced him. 'I could have won the money I need to buy Christmas presents fairly instead of having to borrow it.'

'Lesley, sweetheart, you'd find yourself in debt to me,' he retorted. 'But this talk of betting is an insult.

There's no contest, not when we both want the same outcome.'

'We'll see, shall we?'

'We shall, indeed,' he threatened. 'But now, if you wouldn't mind taking yourself off somewhere far away . . . I was working, remember, when you disturbed me.'

'And nearly brought down on myself a fate worse than death,' she retorted jauntily, preceding him into the centre room with a provocative little swing of her hips.

'A fate worse than death is a lot better than dying, they say,' Rad suggested urbanely.

'I wonder.'

'I wonder . . . if you need to wonder.'

'You had your chance to find out—and lost it,' Lesley reminded him charmingly. 'Yes, Rad, I'm going far away. I shall take to the hills and plot my revenge.'

'Well, be careful,' he adjured abruptly.

'If I'm not at dinner, it means I've decided I can't win and have run away.' She flashed him a brilliant smile.

But the smile faded from her face once she was outside. Almost at once she heard him resume typing.

A small, dry sob escaped her. The act she had put on after realising that, after all, Rad was not going to make love to her fully had drained her considerable reserves of strength, when her every inclination had been to weep with humiliation and hurt.

She literally fled to the hills, making instinctively, blindly, for that dell where, on another occasion, she had been the one to bring a halt to their lovemaking before it could reach its natural conclusion.

But even now she did not weep. She would not! She lay on her back in the soft, short grass, looking up at a shimmering blue sky and hearing, at intervals, thunder grumbling in the distance. The intense heat was oppressive, suffocating, and she felt as if a great, soft weight pressed her down into the ground. Would the storm never come?

Now that sanity was restored to her, if not serenity, she discovered herself to be shocked, not so much by Rad's ultimate rejection of her as by the meaning of her earlier response to him. She had been on fire for him, wantonly begging him to take her; even now she was still tortured by the ache of desire unappeased, and the implications distressed and frightened her.

She couldn't, she couldn't, she couldn't be in love with him!

The idea was so appalling that she thrust it out of her mind as if she had thought something sinful.

With self-control born of desperation, she fell to thinking of the revenge she had sworn to take. And take it she would, rejecting him as he had rejected her. Lesley tried to smile, but her kiss-swollen lips felt stiff.

It was going to be difficult, as she realised with a cold, sinking sensation, feeling little taste for what she was determined to do. Yet she had made a promise, albeit a foolish promise, and she would have to keep it. The risk was to herself, for she would be vulnerable at all times. Somehow she was going to have to make Rad want her so much that he could no longer deny himself, and then she would have to experience again his love-making without succumbing to her own desire, until she was sure that he was sufficiently aroused to feel her rejection of him as the most terrible anguish of his life.

She would do it if it was humanly possible. But first she needed time, time in which to retrain herself in the art of calmness, so she would devote the next few days simply to making a visual impact. Rad's desire for her must grow and grow, and later, when she felt herself adequately in control, she would allow him to initiate the lovemaking which would culminate in her rejection of him.

Lesley wore filmy black at dinner that night and her make-up was even more elaborate than usual. Rad sat opposite her and she allowed a fugitive smile to play briefly about her mouth when her shadowy green eyes rested lingeringly on his tanned face.

He smiled sardonically, as if he knew full well what she was up to . . .

And the next day, too, when she and Shanie accompanied him to Tzaneen, Lesley was once again at her ravishing best, never quite flirting but always on the brink of it, subtly building up the man-woman awareness which already existed far too potently between them.

Her choice of dress that night was devastating, the blood-red of an old-fashioned rose, with one shoulder bare, and she looked a dangerous young woman, with her long slanting eyes full of mystery, and her hair up in the style Rad had once said he liked.

After dinner they sat with the Wards on the cool veranda.

'I can't believe how close we are to Christmas,' Yolande said, as she had been saying for days past. 'This year has gone so fast . . . Shanie's last year at school. Ach, but that makes me feel old!'

'You're such a young mother,' Shanie protested. 'Oh, it will be so nice having Rad and Lesley here for Christmas, won't it?'

'And nicer still for us to be here,' said Rad with a smile. 'I believe I speak for Lesley as well as myself.'

'Yes,' Lesley confirmed quietly, remembering past Christmases and knowing that within this family the celebration would be more like she imagined it ought to be, quieter and simpler than those she had known in

Johannesburg and other places, when heavy drinking, over-eating, over-expensive gifts given even to rivals or enemies and, eventually, frayed tempers and headaches had been the order of the day.

'Especially nice for you, I'm thinking, Rad,' Michael suggested. 'You've been far from home for several Christmases past now.'

'Far from home and often with the sound of gunfire in my ears instead of carols,' Rad admitted, but without bitterness.

Lesley looked at him without the usual eye-tricks then. For a mad moment she felt herself melting, wanting to do something, anything, to make up to him for those bleak working Christmases far, far worse than the most hectic one she had experienced.

She snatched herself back from such weakness, remembering her resolve, but when next she directed her smile at him, she felt nauseated by her own exquisite witchcraft.

'Incidentally,' said Michael a little later, looking from Lesley to Rad, 'we'll be leaving you two alone for two or three days between Christmas and New Year. As you know, I'm without a foreman just now, so we can't go away for a long period, but Yolande has this cousin in Phalaborwa and we're going to stay with her. We wanted to be at home with you for the two celebration days, and she has her own large family, so we're fitting the visit in between the two.'

'Johanna will cook for you—she's quite good—but feel free to mess around in the kitchen if you feel like it, Lesley,' Yolande added. 'You won't feel nervous, staying alone in the house, will you?'

'I could always move into the house with her if she does,' Rad volunteered idly. His eyes were very dark tonight, gleaming with amusement as he met Lesley's glance.

'That won't be necessary,' she assured him with a wicked little smile, and held his gaze for several seconds.

He would wait until the Wards were away, she felt sure, before making love to her again, so she had a few days yet in which to rehearse her rejection of him.

She was distracted by sensing a wave of antipathy so forceful it seemed to pierce her mind, and she turned her head sharply, but Shanie's face was as sweetly simpering as that of the angel she had seen Yolande hang on the tiny Christmas tree indoors.

'Must I go?' Shanie asked her mother in a plaintive voice after a minute. 'Couldn't I stay here with Rad and Lesley?'

'I'm afraid not, Shanie.' Yolande was sympathetic but firm. 'She's your godmother, remember, and with you grown up and going to university, she'll see less and less of you, so I want you to make this visit, please, as a formal thank-you for all the little gifts she's bestowed on you during your schooldays.'

'All right.' Shanie was like a docile child and even smiled lovingly, for which Lesley could only admire her. 'But even just for two or three days . . . Well, I'll miss you, Rad. And you, Lesley,' she added as if she thought the older girl might be hurt at being omitted.

Shortly afterwards Rad got up to go to his rondawel cottage for the night. 'Walk as far as the oak tree with me, Lesley,' he invited easily.

Her long lashes screened her eyes as she stood up, aware once more of Shanie's resentful dislike. They would be within full view of the Wards all the way, so she felt no nervousness about accompanying him.

The garden was a dark place of rustling noises, and above them the navy heavens were crowded with thick clusters of brilliant stars. Rad didn't talk, and neither did Lesley, and the intense heat of the summer night was like an embrace. As they neared the oak tree, Rad slowed his pace a little.

'You're impossibly beautiful, you know,' he said conversationally.

'Thank you,' Lesley responded demurely.

'One of your miraculous smiles, a flutter of your eyelashes and a sideways glance, the perfume of your body . . . They're enough to seduce a man,' he went on reflectively.

'Tell me more.' Lesley moved closer to him so that he should have the full benefit of her perfume.

'But do you need to go to such extreme lengths?' he continued, and suddenly his tone was harshly derogatory. 'You'll wear yourself out with the effort, and it's a waste of energy anyway . . . Quite pointless when, as you know, I already want you.'

'But not enough, Rad, not enough,' she insisted sweetly.

He laughed, and the menacing sound made her shiver.

'I could pity you, Lesley Ann, if I wasn't so absorbed in admiring your incredible act. Because, my dear, when the time comes . . . you're just not going to be able to handle it.'

CHAPTER EIGHT

CHRISTMAS Eve provided a superb setting for Lesley. She, Rad and the Wards attended a party at the country club, but not all the sparkling baubles and masses of flowers adorning the hall, nor all the women as gaudy as butterflies, could vie with her.

'You look like . . . like Christmas,' one of her partners said to her as they danced.

Her dress was made of a softly gleaming silky fabric, a pure, clear crimson, which clung to her graceful body, and its cut was so simple and so effective that every feminine eye in the hall could accurately assess its cost. From her slender neck hung several snakelike strands of silver, fine matching bracelets encircled her wrists, silver glinted from her earlobes and her small dancing feet were encased in feather-light silver sandals which increased her height by several inches. Her silky dark curls had need of no adornment.

Lesley knew she had never looked so good. If she didn't feel the same way, Rad was to blame. He wasn't reacting as he should. He wasn't reacting, period. The evening was nearing its end and he still hadn't asked her to dance. He had danced with Yolande, and a number of attractive local women and, of course, Shanie, debutante-demure in white with pale yellow roses and a flowery perfume.

For the Wards' sakes, because she was their guest, Lesley had behaved with circumspection, refraining from the outrageous flirtation which had been her weapon at Johannesburg parties, relying instead solely on her looks and her impressive number of dancing partners to make the impact she was hoping for.

And Rad had barely looked at her.

As her last partner escorted her back to the table where Rad and Shanie sat alone, since Michael and Yolande had remained on the dance floor waiting for the band to start their next number, Lesley made up her mind.

She sipped at her pink champagne and deliberately caught Rad's glance. He lifted his glass in mocking salute but said nothing.

Lesley's crimson mouth curved enticingly. 'Won't you dance with me, Rad?' she requested gently.

'Yes, Rad.' Shanie looked surprised. 'Now I come to think of it, I don't believe you've danced with Lesley all evening.'

'Now she comes to think of it,' Lesley murmured sarcastically as Rad guided her out on to the dance floor. 'It's my belief that little Shanie came here tonight prepared to keep a tally of how many times you danced with her and how many times with me. She can afford to be generous.'

'Just a little bit jealous, sweetheart?' Rad taunted as he swung her into his arms.

'Just a little.' The sexual tension between them was at such a pitch that Lesley felt faint.

'You haven't lacked for partners,' he reminded her.

Silvered lids concealed her eyes. 'Ah, but did you notice how I kept them all at arm's length?'

'Are you going to do the same to me?'

'No.' She moved her head slightly as she went on huskily, 'Hold me close, Rad, and whisper sweet nothings in my ear. Tomorrow is Christmas Day. Show me a little peace and goodwill.'

'How much goodwill do you feel towards me, I wonder?' he countered perceptively.

But he drew her closer to him until their bodies

touched. It was the closest they had been since that shattering afternoon in his cottage, and Lesley felt sick and dizzy with desire.

She wasn't going to be able to go through with it, she thought with wild panic. But she must! She must carry out her planned revenge. Yet how could she, when Rad affected her like this? Her only consolation at that moment was the fact that he in turn was physically conscious of her, his sensual awareness transmitting itself to her clamant nerves with shocking force.

'You deserve to be beaten,' he muttered, his breath stirring her curls. 'Give it up, Lesley. You'll never bring it off.'

'What are you talking about?'

'You know damned well,' he retorted. 'You're really very frightened, aren't you?'

'Not me,' she said flippantly. 'I'm wild and reckless and as bold as brass.'

'A brazen hussy, in fact.' He laughed mirthlessly. 'No, my dear, you're silly and courageous. You ought to be terrified.'

'Why?'

'Because——' Rad's voice was like frost. 'Because, darling, no woman, however lovely, however desirable, plays games with me and gets away with it. No, don't speak! I don't want to hear another word from you.'

Obediently, Lesley remained silent. Depression dropped over her like a dark mantle and suddenly all she craved was peace, an end to the hostility between them. She yearned to rest against him, and know him kind and compassionate, cradling and comforting her, giving her the understanding she had not known since her grandmother had died.

But tenderness was the one thing she could never expect from Rad Sinclair.

The next morning they all attended an early church service in Duiwelskloof and, after their return to the farm and breakfast, they exchanged gifts in the large, cool lounge.

The day was humid already, with great heavy white clouds banking on the horizon although the sun still shone on the Duiwelskloof area.

'It may miss us, of course,' said Michael. 'But I reckon we can expect a storm either tonight or tomorrow night . . . If the latter, we'll miss it. We're setting off at about mid-morning tomorrow.'

Lesley hoped he was right about a storm. It might do some damage, but it would also put an end to the oppressive heat outside. On their return from church she had changed into a clingy white top, sleeveless and V-necked, and her favourite pair of designer jeans, but now she rather wished she had chosen shorts.

Michael and Yolande were in a romantic mood this morning, exchanging lingering kisses and gazing quietly into each other's eyes, and Lesley looked at them with admiration and a little bewilderment. Such harmony; how did one achieve it?

She turned her attention to the other two. Shanie was in effusive raptures over Lesley's gift of a poster of Sarah Bernhardt and Lesley smiled dismissively.

'I thought it appropriate since you want to be an actress, love.'

'Who could emulate the Divine Sarah?' Shanie was wistful.

'Don't sound so sad; she lost a leg, remember. Settle for being our next Janet Suzman,' Lesley advised, and turned to Rad who was listening to their sweet-voiced exchange with some amusement.

She had kept his present until last and now she held up the tiny gold-wrapped parcel.

'As promised, Rad. It can't compare with these, of

course——' she indicated the tiny emeralds sparkling at her ears '—but it will amuse you.'

'Thank you. It seems to be amusing you considerably,' he commented.

Lesley stood squarely in front of him, looking up into his face with eyes full of charming mischief.

'Open it,' she urged softly.

'I'm not sure if I trust you,' Rad drawled, but his long fingers removed the gold paper to reveal the old jeweller's box in which she had packed the gift.

'No, really . . .' She was nervous and excited and laughing all at once, making no effort to dissemble. 'Oh, you'll laugh at me, I know!'

He paused before opening the box. 'Is that such a bad thing? It's one of your great talents, sweetheart, your ability to amuse.'

He opened the box and as his lean fingers parted the tissue paper inside he looked at her sharply. Then he looked down again, his lips quirking humorously.

'Oh, Lesley,' he said, helpless laughter in his voice.

'I knew you'd laugh!' Yet she was not displeased.

'I might have known, you incredible girl.'

'Do you think I've got a nerve?' she challenged.

'Of course.'

Shanie came to join them. 'What is it?' she asked eagerly.

Rad held it out on the palm of his hand: a stand-up miniature in an antique frame, and the face portrayed in the centre was Lesley's. The artist had faithfully reproduced her lovely delicate skin tints and the living shine of her dark curls, but he had done more than that, for he had managed to capture that half-smiling look of seductive mischief which those who knew her were familiar with. It was the essence of Lesley Ann, glimmering from her eyes and repeated in the poised angle of her head.

Shanie looked momentarily startled, and the look she gave Lesley was unguarded, but she managed to say, 'Gosh, how lovely!'

'It's more than lovely; it's perfect,' said Rad. He sent Lesley a questioning smile. 'Where did you get it? Who did it?'

'A friend . . . I think I do mean a friend, because he was only interested in me from the neck up, rare creature. He was in my class at Varsity and painting miniatures was his hobby.' Lesley laughed, remembering. 'He did me in the canteen one lunchtime and insisted on framing it before giving it to me.'

'A talented young man,' Rad approved. 'Come here and let me thank you properly, Lesley Ann.'

Her lips curved. 'Yolande's artificial mistletoe is at the other end of the room, Rad.'

'I don't need that as an excuse.'

Lesley stepped closer to him and lifted her hands to his shoulders, but he made no move to touch her. 'I wonder what you must be thinking of my vanity in giving you such an egotistical gift?'

'I'm thinking that it's delightfully typical of you,' Rad replied, smiling crookedly.

'But you see,' she went on in a whispery, confiding voice, 'I'm determined that you won't forget me.'

'Who could?' he said simply.

A silence fell and Lesley looked up into his darkly tanned face. 'Have you changed your mind, Rad?'

'No.' He dipped his head and brushed careless lips across her cheek. 'Thank you, lovely Lesley.'

Shaken, she stepped back.

'And thank you for my beautiful earrings, Rad,' she murmured to his shirt-front.

'Think of me when you wear them,' he advised lightly.

She would think of him anyway, she knew despairingly. And why, oh, why were they talking as if their parting was imminent and inevitable? Simply because it was, the answer came to her immediately.

Lesley turned away and the bright room swam before her eyes. Yolande had used real holly leaves for her floral decorations, but since they were berryless she had added tapering scarlet candles surrounded by poinsettia flowers and red geraniums.

'You must be like me, Lesley.' Yolande's cool hand on her arm was soothing. 'I also get all emotional at Christmas. Come to the kitchen with me. I have to see to my turkey.'

In this bright, hot part of Africa, the Wards adhered to English and Continental tradition in the way they celebrated Christmas, with a few South African touches, such as bright pink watermelon, thrown in to make of it something quite individual and delightful.

Lesley took quiet pleasure in it all. It was so much simpler, and closer to the true spirit of the festival, than the Christmases she had known. Seeing Rad relaxed and in an easygoing mood, she knew that he too appreciated it, probably even more than she did.

She had temporarily abandoned the ultra-seductive manner which had characterised her in recent days. This was Christmas Day and surely no occasion to be pursuing revenge. Besides which, she was feeling intensely vulnerable just now and doubted if she had the heart to carry this thing through to its planned conclusion.

But that night she was recalled to the need for an act. She was sitting, solitary, on the veranda, as still as a statue in an effort to keep cool. A little earlier, stormclouds had gathered over the farm and thunder had rumbled, but they drifted away without shedding their load and the night was almost as hot as the day had been.

Shanie had gone upstairs to pack in readiness for the

following day's departure for Phalaborwa, while Rad had remained in the lounge with Yolande and Michael.

Now, however, he came out on to the veranda, and stood looking down at her in brooding silence. Lesley didn't stir in the cane chair. Since they had eaten a midday dinner today, the evening meal had been a snack supper beside the pool, so she was still in her jeans but after swimming that afternoon she had put on a fresh top. With nothing worn under it, this one was cool, permitting the few occasional wisps of breeze that stirred to caress her warm skin. A startling flamingo pink, it was constructed of a number of semi-transparent triangles hung from two thin shoulder straps.

'Come.' Rad held out his hand to her. 'Walk with me for a while.'

Lesley stood up but didn't take his hand. She knew, without wondering or speculation, what his motive was. He wasn't going to wait until after the Wards' departure. Presently he would start making love to her and ask her to come with him to his cottage, and then . . . Then she would say her piece and it would all be over.

What would happen after that, Lesley couldn't surmise, and she kept such questions at bay by concentrating resolutely on the immediate present.

She felt breathless as she walked through the still garden beside him. Her greatest performance ever was called for, and she knew the odds against her being able to give it.

'What were you thinking about back there?' Rad asked idly.

'About . . . oh, today, I suppose,' she confessed hesitantly. 'This is the nicest Christmas I've had; nearly perfect.'

'Nearly, but not quite,' he said with a certain derisive humour. 'But it will be, sweetheart.'

'That's up to you, isn't it?' she challenged sweetly.

'I suppose so,' he conceded ironically. 'But first tell me—have you thought about your parents today?'

'Not really.' Lesley was a little surprised. 'Are they worth it? But I suppose I should have been wondering how they were spending today.'

'Why should you?' he retorted shortly.

'I don't suppose this Christmas was any inferior to all their others,' she went on musing with a trace of bitterness. 'And believe me, Rad, they were never austere. No, they'll have been drinking and eating and my mother will have another jewellery case to add to her collection, crammed full of gorgeous things . . . It's scum that always rises to the top, isn't it?'

'I'm regretting I brought the subject up,' Rad said expressionlessly.

'No, but parents are funny things when you really think about them,' Lesley insisted, driven by a strange regretful mood which cast all other thoughts from her mind. 'They influence us——'

'Possibly,' he interrupted harshly. 'But they can neither make nor break most of us, Lesley. Remember that.'

'Do you mean that had my parents been like, say, Yolande and Michael, I'd still be exactly as I am?' she questioned him curiously.

'Well, you certainly wouldn't be a Shanie,' he laughed.

'God forbid,' Lesley said fervently.

'Oh, I've no doubt that your parents may have influenced—or rather, affected you a little,' Rad went on. 'But you, out of all people, Lesley, have the strength to rise above your parents.'

'I think perhaps that other . . . things have influenced me to a greater extent than my parents,' she suggested thoughtfully. 'Would you believe, Rad, that until I was sixteen I was quite nice?'

She felt him glance at her in the darkness. 'You can also rise above those other influences if you really want to.'

'I thought I had. After all, I know myself to be superior to . . . to . . .'

'To all those men who've had you,' he supplied.

'To all those men who've wanted me,' Lesley corrected him hopelessly.

'Of course.' His voice gave nothing away.

She would have liked him to believe the truth, she thought wistfully as they walked on in silence, but it was too late now. He would never be given the chance to find out for himself.

They were some distance from the house now, and as they passed between an Australian flame tree and a bauhinia, Rad came to a halt.

'All right, let's get it over with, Lesley,' he said curtly.

'What?' She was startled by both the words and his tight, furious tone.

'This is what you've been after, isn't it?'

He jerked her roughly against him, his mouth descending on hers in brutal assault, and Lesley didn't even have time for a gasp of surprise.

Rad showed her no mercy, straining her against him until she felt she must break, while he continued to bruise her mouth with savage kisses which actually hurt her.

'Oh, God, Rad, not like this,' she moaned entreatingly when her mouth was free for a moment.

'How, then?' he demanded hoarsely.

'You're hurting me,' she gasped.

'That's all you deserve, sweetheart,' he retorted, and

fastened his mouth to hers again in yet another painful kiss.

Her lips felt raw and her body bruised, yet even as he continued to humiliate her with his lack of tenderness or respect, Lesley thrilled to the warmth of his body and was carried away on a dark tide of desire.

Somehow her arms were tight about his neck, her fingers entwined in his hair, and scorching passion shot through her body. All thought of revenge had gone. This was basic and entirely elemental, this need that seared her and which only his penetration could assuage.

'Lesley . . . Lesley!'

Subtly, Rad's mood had shifted from punishing anger to something else that she couldn't quite define. He drew back from her a little, thrusting his hands beneath her flimsy top and then lowering his head to drop kisses on her shoulders. Lesley's breasts tautened at his touch, but then his hands were sliding round to her back, magically caressing, and her body was against the hard length of his once more.

'Enough, Lesley,' he muttered huskily against the side of her neck.

'Not enough,' she moaned softly, arching her body against his in wanton invitation.

'But yes,' he contradicted her. 'Haven't we got to the stage where I ask you to come back to the cottage and go to bed with me . . . and then you denounce me with a chilling little speech and one of your coolest smiles?'

Lesley grew very still.

'Isn't that the scenario?' he persisted silkily.

He held her away from him, his hands encircling her arms just above the elbows.

'Oh, God.' Lesley's voice was low and defeated.

Rad's hands moved lightly up and down her arms.

'Come on, sweetheart, get it over with. Say your piece.'

'I . . . I can't.'

Lesley wanted to collapse against him. She felt weak, drained of every vestige of strength. How could she have forgotten? But even now, mingled with her humiliation at being caught out, was the warmth of relief.

'Sure?'

She nodded. 'Yes.'

'All right, then.' Rad relaxed and his hands fell away from her arms. 'We'll forget about it. Just don't be so stupid again. You couldn't have gone through with it, you know.'

'I know,' she sighed helplessly, swaying slightly.

'Are you all right?' Rad asked sharply.

'Yes.' Her answer was a whisper.

'Sure? I'm sorry I was so rough with you,' he went on. 'I hadn't intended to be, but I was just so furious with you for dreaming up such a foul plot that I could think of nothing but making you pay for it. It wasn't worthy of you, Lesley.'

'It's all right.' She was glad, glad that she had been prevented from carrying out her revenge. 'I'm sorry, Rad. You deserved better of me.'

'Yes, and I shall have better of you some time,' he said quietly. 'And you of me, Lesley.'

It sounded like a promise and Lesley strained her eyes in an attempt to read his face in the dark.

'Come. I'll take you back to the house now,' he said after a short silence.

His hand at her back was a comfort and Lesley felt at peace as they walked back, which was strange, considering all that had just occurred.

She said tentatively, 'Rad, how did you know I . . . I wouldn't be able to carry out what I'd planned?'

'I know you, you see,' he told her amusedly. 'That's why I thought I'd better remind you of your intentions before things got really out of hand.'

'But why should you? You could have—I was——'

'Think what you'd have thought of yourself tomorrow,' he adjured her. 'Leave it alone for now, Lesley. It's not important.'

They completed the walk back to the house in silence and halted below the veranda.

'I won't come in again,' Rad told her. 'Goodnight, Lesley.'

'Rad . . .'

He shook his head. 'Not yet, Lesley. I've got a miniature portrait of you now, remember.'

'Hardly an adequate substitute for the original model, I would have thought?' she challenged mischievously.

'Nothing quells you for long, does it?' he laughed. 'I can wait, but I promise to look at your image before I go to bed tonight. Have I got it right . . . the sweet nonsense of romance?'

Lesley smiled, more moved than she had ever been. No man had ever spoken to her like this before; no man had ever been prepared to wait . . .

'You've got it perfectly,' she assured him. 'But you know, Rad, I don't really need it . . . not now.'

'I'd like you to be sure of that.' Rad laid his hands on her shoulders and bent his head to kiss her gently on the mouth. 'That's to make up for those other . . . I can't call them kisses. Go inside now, Lesley.'

'Yes. Goodnight, Rad.'

She moved up on to the veranda, knowing that he watched her, and turned at the door. They exchanged smiles, and Lesley's was probably the first completely spontaneous smile she had ever given him. Then Rad turned and walked away towards the rondawel cottage.

Lesley watched him go. She wanted to run after him and beg him to take her with him, but she knew that he would turn her away tonight. But he would not always turn her away. Soon now, perhaps very soon, he would want to make her his, and when that time came, if it was tomorrow, or in the new year, she would be ready for him, ready to give herself to him. All of herself, her heart as well as her body.

Because she loved Rad Sinclair.

Lesley went into the house and shut the door quietly. She felt buoyed up by something wonderful and completely new to her, and she seemed to drift rather than walk upstairs.

In her room she lay down on her bed, merely revelling in the discovery she had made. She treasured her new self-knowledge and recognised it as the most precious thing that had ever come her way.

From the room next door came a few experimental chords of music as Shanie strummed her guitar. Lesley stared up at the ceiling, her lips curving tenderly.

It didn't matter that Rad didn't love her; she couldn't expect that. She thought he probably cared about her, though, else why would he have behaved as he had done tonight? But she dared not be too sure about that even, so new and unexpected was this wonderful thing.

At last, reluctantly, she got up off the bed and went to run herself a bath. She sat in the scented water for a long time. She would begin to soap herself and then fall to dreaming, again and again. Rad had said he would look at the miniature she had given him before he went to bed. She wondered if he would remember. If he did, he would smile, but perhaps only a little mockingly.

Lesley only roused herself when the water grew too cold to be comfortable, and even later, with her nightly beauty routine completed, she felt reluctant to go to sleep, although she got into bed and switched out her bedside lamp. All she wanted to do was lie here, quite happily, and think about Rad, anticipating the time when he would claim her.

He wanted her, and perhaps he cared about her just a little. Loving for the first time ever, she felt her heart flooded with the emotion. She yearned to give and give to him, her beloved, all that he asked of her, and certainly the time would come when he must ask something of her.

But that time might be a while in coming, she realised resignedly the next day. Rad was in one of his distant, abstracted moods at breakfast, and still equally remote when he reappeared later to say goodbye to the Wards when they left for Phalaborwa.

'I think you're going to be lonely, Lesley,' Yolande laughed. 'I can see Rad is in a mood to be getting on with some work—on Boxing Day of all days.'

'I think that storm will break late this afternoon or tonight,' said Michael as he and Rad joined them.

Yolande looked up at the sky sceptically. The usual white clouds were missing, blindingly brilliant with the sun shining on them.

'You and your storm, Michael!' she teased. 'You've made up your mind that there's going to be one . . . We'll come back to find it hasn't happened yet and you'll go on predicting it all summer.'

Michael shook his head. 'We're not in a drought year. Those aren't the spite-clouds that come to mock farmers in the bad times. There's definitely something building up.'

'Oh, well, have it your own way,' Yolande gave in. She turned to Rad and Lesley. 'We'll be home on the afternoon of the twenty-ninth, you two.'

'Look after each other,' Michael adjured lightly as he opened his car door and prepared to get in.

'I do wonder what that means, Mike?' Rad laughed with a sardonic glance for Lesley.

'Whatever you want it to mean,' Michael said airily.

'That gives us a lot of choice!'

'Now there you surprise me.'

This exchange was beyond Lesley—but perhaps not beyond Shanie, because one of those sudden almost tangible blasts of hostility came at her from the girl.

As the car disappeared from sight, Rad turned to Lesley.

'You'll survive without me, won't you?' he queried.

'No,' Lesley said simply.

He laughed. 'I only meant for today. I'd like to do some work. Ask Johanna to bring me a sandwich or something at one o'clock and I'll see you at dinner tonight.'

'As you wish,' Lesley promised demurely, concealing her disappointment.

He smiled at her. 'There'll be time for us, Lesley.'

But his obvious lack of anxiety that that time should be soon revealed to her the difference between his feelings and hers. She returned to the house, thinking about it. He wanted her but could wait until other more important things no longer occupied his time and attention, whereas she loved him and wanted the fulfilment of that love now . . . and always.

But she would not demand it. She must not expect too much, she knew. She would be satisfied with whatever he chose to give, when he chose to give it. Or would she be the only one to do the giving, and he be the recipient? That too she must accept.

She prepared his lunch herself, but since he had said that Johanna should take it to him, Johanna it would be, and the maid went down to the rondawel cottage with the tray. Lesley had no intention of risking his displeasure by intruding when she was not wanted.

She swam after her own lunch, but presently a cloud passed over the sun. Michael could be right about his storm, she reflected, noting how the clouds had changed from white to leaden grey. They had moved in closer now too, but the day remained intensely hot with not a leaf stirring in the garden.

Inside, Lesley joined Johanna in the kitchen and took over the making of a cold dessert for dinner that night. When next she looked out, the clouds had turned to purple, but they needed to come a great deal closer in before there was a chance of a storm.

By evening, however, the atmosphere was decidedly thundery. It made Lesley uneasy, prey to a fey certainty that something cataclysmic was about to happen, but whether good or bad, she could not sense. She remembered her feeling of relentless destiny approaching on that evening of another storm, that evening she had met Rad . . .

The memory caused her to choose to wear the black dress she had worn then, but if Rad recognised it when he came up to the house for dinner, he gave no sign.

He was still in a thoughtful mood, friendly in an absent sort of way, but disinclined to talk. Lesley was unperturbed and made no attempt to alter the tone of the evening. She knew by now that his work was something he set apart from the rest of his life, because it had first claim on him.

She vowed that she would be whatever he wanted her to be: quiet when he would have her so, amusing when he was in a mood to be entertained, sensual when he had a physical need of her.

Tonight he wanted her quiet. But all the time, there was an ache torturing both her body and heart, springing from her hungry need to be fully united with him.

He didn't stay long after the meal was over.

'Mike's storm is about to drop in on us,' he said, pausing at the front door. 'Make sure all windows are fastened before you go to bed. Goodnight, Lesley.'

Then, to her surprise, he turned her into his arms and kissed her lingeringly and gently on the mouth. Their lips clung, but now he was turning from her.

'Rad?' Lesley's voice was low and strained, full of the pain of her longing for him.

'Don't make it difficult for me, Lesley,' he requested tautly. 'I'm trying to give you time. Don't you realise that?'

Then he was gone from her, into a grape-black night soon to erupt into a ferocious storm, and the front door slammed behind him.

Limp, Lesley sat down on the stairs. Time, he had said. If only he could know of the agony tormenting her, he would know that time was not what she needed.

CHAPTER NINE

JOHANNA had retired to her quarters for the night and Lesley was alone in the house. She had gone through every room checking windows, and then gone to her bedroom.

So much for her feeling that something must happen tonight, she thought bleakly. The storm was all that would happen.

With no one to look at her, she removed all her make-up in order to give her skin a chance to breathe, switched on the transistor radio Shanie had lent her soon after her arrival, tuning it to a music station, and settled down with a novel, thinking that she might switch off the light and watch the storm when it arrived later.

At about half-past nine the telephone rang in the hall.

Barefooted, Lesley ran downstairs to answer it. She couldn't remember the number, so she simply said, 'This is the Wards' farm.'

'Oh!' The male voice suggested that its owner had been concentrating on something else while he waited for an answer and that she had surprised him. 'Oh! Look, is it possible for me to speak to Rad Sinclair tonight?'

'Well . . .' Lesley hesitated, 'I suppose I could go and fetch him for you. He's not in the house, you see.'

'No, I know about the cottage he has. No, please don't trouble yourself. For once it's nothing urgent, but if you could give him a message when you see him?'

'Of course.' Lesley looked about her for a pencil.

'Thanks a lot,' the voice said briskly. 'It's just this—ask him to contact his newspaper some time during tomorrow. Okay?'

'Is that all?'

'That's all,' he confirmed cheerfully. 'Thanks. 'Bye now.'

He rang off and Lesley put the receiver down slowly, amused by his haste and wondering who he was. Some sort of editor, probably, news, features, political? She didn't even know who Rad was answerable to on his paper, she realised. She had a lot to learn about him yet.

She went into the dark lounge and parted the curtains at the front window. She could see the lights of Rad's cottage. A strong wind was starting up now, stirring the garden into movement, and lightning flickered threateningly.

If she ran down to the cottage now and gave him the message, she would just have time to get back to the house before the heavy, restless clouds deposited their burden.

Lesley knew it wasn't necessary, but just to see Rad one more time tonight . . . The message was an excuse.

Not stopping to don shoes, she didn't think coherently again until she had shut the front door behind her. As she left the veranda the wind tugged at her with cool ruthlessness, almost pulling her over, and she paused for a moment to gather her strength. It was so strong now that it was bending a tall bottlebrush tree right over and ripping flower-heads from their stalks. The night was full of violent sound, the shrieking of the wind and the deafening claps of thunder which were coming immediately after the jagged streaks of lightning which rent the turbulent sky.

Lesley ran through the garden, glad now of her lack of shoes, for they would have slowed her. The wind whipped the skirt of her dress about her legs. She reached the cottage and collapsed breathlessly against the closed door for a moment, then straightened and thrust it open without bothering to knock.

Shirtless and barefoot, as he preferred to be when working, Rad was seated in front of the typewriter at his desk, but he swung round at her entry and stood up as he saw her.

'Lesley! You crazy creature.' Anger appeared on his face. 'What's wrong?'

'Nothing,' Lesley gasped, slamming the door shut against the raging turmoil of the night.

'Then what are you doing here?' he demanded.

'A message.' She laughed selfconsciously. 'It could have waited, I know, but——'

'What message?' he interrupted, instantly alert.

'From your newspaper,' she explained. 'You're to telephone them some time tomorrow.'

'Was that all?' There was a wary look about his eyes now.

'Yes. He said it wasn't all that urgent. I don't know who he was,' she added.

Rad relaxed. 'They probably want some sort of feature, perhaps a forecast for Africa in the new year. We've discussed it before. But Lesley, you mad thing, you needn't have come out in this wind. Tomorrow would have done.'

'I know,' she admitted with a faint smile. 'Hell seems to be up in heaven tonight. I'll have to run back or I'm going to get soaked.'

Rad wasn't listening. He was staring at her face with mocking amusement glinting in his eyes.

'Can I tell you something?' His lips quirked irresistibly. 'You've come out not only without your shoes, but without your make-up.'

'Oh!' Lesley's hands flew to her cheeks. 'I forgot!

Don't look at me, please, Rad.'

'Why not?' He laughed, his fingers encircling her wrists and pulling her hands away from her face. 'I've seen you unadorned before, remember . . . and very lovely too.'

Disconcerted, she stared up into his face while his eyes, darkened suddenly until they were almost black, caressed the creamy pallor of her face and lingered on the rosy curve of her unpainted mouth.

'Very, very lovely,' he repeated in a disturbing tone. 'Too lovely . . . Lesley, you've got to get out of here; get back to the house before all hell breaks loose. Off you go!'

He turned her in the direction of the door, giving her a gentle push with one hand while opening the door with the other. Lesley stared up at the boiling sky in dismay.

'I'll have to run.'

The first warm heavy drops of moisture were beginning to thud on to the earth.

'The horses?' she wondered.

'Baptist had orders to stable them,' Rad reassured her, raising his voice as a deafening explosion of thunder came almost simultaneously with the flash of sheet lightning which had turned the garden to a frightening blanched violet place for a long moment. 'You can't go out in this, Lesley.'

'I can just make it.'

'If you don't get struck by lightning,' he derided tautly. 'It's directly overhead now.'

Even as he spoke the drops of rain gave way to the first of the deluge and Lesley shrank back because the rain was pouring down, coming in great sheets of water as if a celestial dam had burst.

'You'll have to wait until it's over,' said Rad, pulling her back into the room and shutting the door firmly.

Suddenly, impulsively, he drew her against him, and his voice had roughened. 'Stay with me tonight, Lesley! I wanted to give you time to be sure, my darling, but I can't wait any longer. I must have you, so stay with me.'

Lesley's eyes were dark green but very clear, and very confident as she looked up into his tense face. Her arms slid round him. 'I'll stay with you, Rad.'

She felt the tremor that ran through him as their lips met and instantly she felt her blood stirring into vibrant, singing life. Their mouths became a single entity, a whirling vortex of hunger.

'Be very sure, my darling,' he urged, sliding his hands down her back and then caressing her hips.

'I am sure,' she told him in a voice that shook with the intensity of her emotion. 'Oh, Rad, didn't you know . . . there was no need to wait?'

A single lamp burned in the bedroom. Lesley couldn't remember how they had got there, but Rad had undressed her and himself with quick expertise and now his hands caressed her body with fiercely passionate intimacy while his lips plundered her full throbbing breasts. Their bodies gleamed in the soft light.

'Trust me, Lesley Ann,' he murmured reassuringly, drawing her up and up through ascending levels of desire towards the point of ultimate surrender.

'I do. Oh, Rad, my darling, I love you,' she moaned brokenly, arching against him. 'I love you so very much.'

'Oh, God,' he groaned under the weight of his desire, his body tense and vital, hard against her softness. 'What you can do to a man, Lesley! Touch me, love me!'

His voice became hoarse and inarticulate now, his murmurings interspersed with Lesley's frenzied declarations of love. Outside the storm raged, cooling the earth, but inside all was torrid warmth.

'Don't be frightened, my darling, it will be all right.' His lips stilled the trembling of hers.

And it was all right. As he conquered her instinctive tensing, Lesley couldn't suppress a sharp gasp of pain, but after that everything was so easy and she felt as if she could die of this exquisite pleasure. The thrusting of his loins pleasured her, eased her, and she clung to him, her nails digging into his shoulders as she moaned her rapturous delight in the strange new voice of a woman possessed.

Outside the cottage the storm still shrieked and howled, rising to a furious crescendo of sound; within, Lesley's strangled little cries of love filled the room as Rad brought her to the ultimate shuddering ecstasy, and then she sobbed in his arms as the final spasm of rapture convulsed her.

Then afterwards she was enfolded in Rad's strong arms and there were no words exchanged as their breathing returned to normal. With her cheek pressed against Rad's chest, Lesley listened to the beat of his heart gradually slowing into rhythm again. Peace, rich and deep and full, enveloped her and she had no wish to move. Their bodies were close, touching each other, and she knew from the relaxed stillness of his that she had not failed him, but had given to him just as completely as he had given to her.

A sheet covered them now. It hadn't been there before and she wondered who had pulled it up. She was sure she hadn't.

Eventually she let her head slip back until she could look into his face. Her slanting eyes were luminous with joy. Rad was still awake, but his face was more relaxed than she had ever seen it, and she couldn't suppress a quiver of wonderment. She had done this for him.

He saw her looking at him and his mouth curved, the expression in his eyes miraculously tender as he held her gaze.

'Are you all right?'

'Yes,' Lesley said simply with a little break in her voice.

'Do you want the light out?'

'No. I want to look at you,' she confided with a slow, radiant smile, while slight colour flowed attractively into her cheeks.

Rad's smile deepened and he shifted slightly until he could cradle her head with one hand, his fingers entwined in the dark tangle of her curls.

'I've a confession to make, my darling,' he said tenderly. 'I only half believed you when you claimed to be a virgin. Now I know . . . I'm sorry I hurt you.'

Lesley's lips parted against his left shoulder, her tongue touching the healed bullet wound. 'Do you honestly think that tiny moment of pain can stand up against . . . all the rest?' she asked him in a voice shivery with emotion.

Rad kissed her gently on her brow. 'You're wonderful,' he murmured.

'So are you,' Lesley sighed contentedly.

There was another silence, then she moved one hand to touch his chest, stroking the fine dark hairs and tugging at them lovingly.

'What are you doing?' Rad asked idly. 'Witch woman . . . and my darling. There was never another like you. Did you know the storm would force you to stay here?'

'I suppose I . . . hoped,' she admitted candidly. 'But I didn't consciously admit it to myself.'

His lips were touching her temple now and she felt him smile.

'And you once thought you were frigid,' he mocked gently.

'I don't believe I was, really, do you?' Lesley's eyes were worshipping as she drew back to smile at him. 'I was just waiting for you, that's all.'

'Or someone like me,' he suggested.

'No, just you. I love you, Rad,' she said clearly, and felt his arms come closely about her, tightening as he muttered something inaudible while she continued murmuring of her love. She felt it flowing from her in a great warm torrent and knew she could never give him enough.

Later he turned to her again, his hands moving with incredible tenderness over her swelling breasts and flat belly until her desire flared again and she reponded to him passionately, knowing how best to please him and, a little later, crying out for him to take her, unable to delay any longer that fulfilment of her endless need for him. If anything, the second time was even more excitingly satisfying than the first, since on this occasion there was no moment of pain for Lesley, and again and again she cried aloud her love for him.

Then afterwards, their whispered endearments dying away into silence, the room now in darkness and the storm outside having abated, they fell into a sated sleep, their limbs still entwined, but totally relaxed now.

But some hours later when Lesley awoke, she sensed at once that Rad was no longer relaxed. The darkness was just beginning to lighten into greyness and she couldn't see him at all clearly. He was still asleep, but moving restlessly about, his arms flung out, and she sensed some deep distress.

'Rad.' She laid a hand on his arm, hoping the touch would calm him, but it didn't, and he continued to stir protestingly, muttering too rapidly for her to understand.

Lesley's eyes strove to pierce the gloom. She was stricken with pain at the realisation that even after their tumultuous lovemaking he could still find himself stranded in the midst of some dark and terrible dream. It hurt her to know that he was suffering, and she unable to share his anguish with him.

'The children! The children!' Rad's voice, suddenly coherent, was agonised.

'Rad—wake!' Lesley shook him urgently, desperate to free him from whatever was torturing him. 'Wake up, my darling!'

He tensed, very still suddenly, then relaxed, his hands reaching out for her.

'Lesley Ann?'

'Yes.' She raised herself on one elbow to lean over him, stroking his face with the fingers of her free hand and finding it moist with perspiration. She inclined her head, her curls falling about his face, and kissed him gently. 'All right now?'

'I was dreaming, wasn't I?' Rad expelled a long sigh and pulled her down to him so that she lay half across him. 'I've been waking at about this time every morning since I started my leave . . . waking from some dream that I can never remember. I only know that it's a bad one.'

'You were . . . you said something about the children,' she tried to help him. 'You sounded . . . oh, I don't know—appalled, I think.'

'Oh, my God,' he said quietly, his arms tightening about her.

'What children, my darling?'

He seemed to hesitate. 'Lesley . . . I think I know now. But, darling, I can't lay that on you.'

'You can, you know,' she reassured him softly. 'It's what I'm here for. No matter how terrible it is . . . and it is, isn't it? Something you've seen.'

'Yes.' Another sigh escaped him. 'Most of the things I see in the course of my job . . . well, it's my job, to observe objectively, and I can manage it most of the time. But everywhere I've been I've had to see too the children as victims of war, politics and sometimes famine or disaster, and that's what I've never been able to take. I think it's the stark incomprehension of the younger ones that gets to me most. They don't understand.'

There, in that still dawn hour with the grey light gradually filling the room, Lesley held Rad to her and heard about the children whose plight had filled him with such anguish and rage, children all over Africa, in Chile, Afghanistan, the children among the boat people of Vietnam, children in Biafra, Bangladesh, Belfast, Palestine . . .

And she stroked his face and hair, and wept for him the tears he would never shed, and when they made love again there was a new tender quality to their coming together this time, in a union infused with complete understanding, a oneness of spirit which melted Lesley with the knowledge that her love for Rad was for ever.

They slept very late that morning, finally emerging to find Johanna entirely unperturbed by their failure to appear at the normal breakfasting hour, having drawn her own accurate conclusions when she had discovered Lesley's bed to be unslept in.

The sun was shining from a clear blue sky and there was no trace left of the thunder which had made the atmosphere heavy for so long past. Instead, the world had a bright, newly washed look about it, cleaned and freshened by the rain, and Rad and Lesley spent a leisurely day, mostly outside. They talked and were silent, touching frequently, and when their eyes met they smiled at each other without reserve.

There was no thought of Rad's working, but at some time during the course of the day, Lesley reminded him, 'You're supposed to telephone your paper.'

'Why bring that up?' he asked ruefully, but a little later he reluctantly left her to go and make the call.

He looked thoughtful when he rejoined her beside the pool a short while later.

'You've got to do some work?' Lesley guessed.

'No.' He shook his head and smiled down at her. 'It wasn't important.'

'I'm glad.'

'So am I.' He pulled her up against him, his arms encircling her bikini-clad body. 'I just want to be with my woman . . . my incredible woman.'

His kiss was deep and contained such a fine degree of passion that tears stood in Lesley's eyes and finally spilled over on to her cheeks when they parted.

'Crying, my darling?' Rad kissed the salty wetness away.

'Silly, am I not?' She gave him a dazzling smile now. 'But I'm so very much in love with you, Rad, that it overwhelms me at moments like these.'

And his embrace tightened while his lips sought hers again.

Their time together had an idyllic, honeymoon quality. Lesley never once thought of the future, never wondered what would happen later. She lived only for the present, devoting every thought to Rad. Their relationship was a harmonious blend of laughter and tenderness and passion. She welcomed equally the quiet moments and those exciting moments when his surging desire would make him turn to her, his need kindling her own.

The sunlit days, when Johanna and Baptist discreetly avoided them, and the warm dark nights spent together filled Lesley with a happiness she hadn't known was possible, and she knew that Rad too had given himself up to this idyll as completely as she had done. She rejoiced in the differences between them; man and woman, hard and meltingly soft.

'I feel I could die, when we're together like that,' he told her in the darkness of the night after he had once again filled her with indescribable rapture. '*Liebestod* ... Do you know that word? Death by love ... Oh, God, Lesley!'

'Rad ... Rad!' It was a threnody of joy. 'I'm glad I was able to give you so much.'

'So much and so much, my darling.' He held her very close. 'You're perfect. You give all the time, and it makes you so strong and sure and generous ... all woman. My woman.'

He was troubled by no further dreams on the nights following that first one, and she knew that this too she had done for him by enabling him to talk about what had haunted him.

After their third night together, he bent over her, his hands at the sides of her face, caressing, gently stroking back her curls. She had already been up to make coffee in the opposite rondawel at the other end of the cottage's central room, and they had drunk it in bed and relaxed against the pillows, not talking very much, preferring to simply look at each other.

'Do you know the date?' Rad questioned her now with a smile.

'The twenty-ninth ... oh!' Lesley looked at him uncertainly and knew a pang of regret.

'I'm afraid so. They'll get back some time this afternoon.' He paused, searching her face intently before dropping a kiss on the corner of her mouth. 'Lesley, this is too perfect a thing to be lied about and concealed, and I can't give you up now ... So I want you to move in here with me. I notice a great many of your possessions have already found their way down here, but you can pack up later today and move in properly. I'll explain to Mike and Yolande.'

'Rad . . . oh, thank you!' Relief made her smile up at him.

'The situation won't embarrass you?' he asked.

Her fingertips traced the outline of his lips and he kissed them swiftly, his tongue caressing.

'No, it won't embarrass me,' she whispered.

'And you can be sure it won't embarrass the Wards,' he promised her. 'They'll understand.'

How could they fail to? she thought. How could anyone expect him to deny himself that which he needed, remembering to what it was that he must shortly return? The intrusion of reality chilled Lesley and she found herself clinging to him.

'Make love to me, Rad,' she beseeched him shamelessly. 'Just once more like this, before we have to think of other people. Love me!'

Instantly attuned to her need, he brought his body over hers and she felt his desire flare to harmonise with her own flagrant longing.

'Oh, my God, I'll never stop wanting you, Lesley,' he groaned urgently with mounting hunger.

She welcomed his rigid maleness with a glad gasp, but there was a quality of desperation in the way she clung to him because it had come to her that something was approaching which would end all this. So fine, so highly pitched was this conviction that it raised their joining to exquisite heights from which she might have toppled over into despairing agony had Rad not been controlling her, bending her to his will as he stifled her cries with his mouth.

'What was that all about, my darling?' he asked a little later.

Lesley was still shaken. 'I'm scared,' she murmured

brokenly. 'Something is going to happen. I can feel it.'

He might have mockingly dismissed her fears, but he didn't. Instead he searched her face with eyes that darkened as he noted how highly strung and taut she seemed this morning.

'You really are fey, aren't you?' he sighed eventually. 'I can feel your fear, and I'm not dismissing it lightly, my darling, but I just can't see what can happen. Have faith . . . in us, Lesley. We won't let anything happen.'

'I pray that you may be right,' she told him gravely.

'I am,' he assured her. His lips moved gently over her cheek, then he drew back to look at her. 'God! You're more beautiful this morning than I've ever seen you.'

'I think it's because I'm . . . whole . . . complete,' she suggested.

'As I am. You've given me everything, Lesley,' he said seriously. Then a tender smile lit his face. 'It's not a thing to cry about, my darling.'

Rad sent her into the main house to pack in the afternoon, and Lesley was still busy when she heard the sound of the Wards' car stopping outside. She hesitated, feeling a little shy, and hoped Rad would lose no time in explaining the situation to them. They would, of course, understand. Well, Michael and Yolande would, but Shanie? She realised that she hadn't thought about the girl once during the time she had been absent. Shanie would be upset and resentful, of course, but surely she couldn't cause any trouble?

Yet Lesley still couldn't free herself of the conviction that somehow her time of joy was ending.

Nobody had yet entered the house when she emerged from the bedroom and, as she descended the stairs, she was startled by the telephone ringing in the hall below.

Yolande and Michael must still be out at the car, because nobody came to answer it, nor had anyone appeared by the time Lesley reached it.

'Hullo, the Wards' farm,' she said pleasantly, glancing through the open door to the driveway where she could see Yolande standing by while Michael and Baptist unloaded the car's boot. She had expected Rad to be out there with them, but perhaps he hadn't heard their arrival if he was in the cottage.

And Shanie wasn't to be seen either. Lesley's lips curved ruefully. Shanie had probably gone running off to the cottage to greet Rad . . . as she had greeted him that other time? Something twisted within Lesley.

'Hi there!' She remembered the voice and smiled. 'I think I spoke to you the other night?'

'Yes . . . that's Rad's paper again, isn't it?'

'Right.' He laughed. 'I suppose he's holed up in his cottage again?'

'Well, he's not here at the moment but, once again, I could go and fetch him for you,' she volunteered.

'And once again, don't trouble,' he begged her. 'If you'd just deliver another message? It's quite simple, Mrs Ward—or are you the daughter? You sound young. Look, please tell Rad that we really could do with that story on the Crosnier girl now, okay?'

Not a sound escaped her, but the knuckles of the hand holding the receiver were white.

'Hullo? Are you still there?' the man's voice persisted. 'Did you get that?'

'Yes . . . yes.' Lesley swallowed painfully. 'Is that all?'

'That's all,' he confirmed. 'He'll understand. We discussed it when he called back two days ago . . . With Gerard Crosnier apparently vanished off the face of the earth, the story is dying, and we'd like to keep it alive a little longer.'

'I'll tell him,' she got out through stiff lips.

'Thanks a lot.'

She put the receiver down and stared at the wall. She felt cold, icy cold. Frost numbed her nerves and spread through her bones. She kept her lips compressed lest her grief and rage find an outlet in the anguished scream that was filling her mind.

She moved slowly. She knew what to do. She crossed the hall and emerged on the veranda just as Yolande was coming up the steps.

'Hullo, Lesley,' Yolande greeted her warmly. 'Has everything been all right? Shanie has gone to say hullo to Rad. Why, Lesley! What's wrong? Lesley . . . Lesley, come back!'

But Lesley was brushing past her in silence, her eyes blazing, but blazing with such an icy light that Yolande fell back fearfully.

She wouldn't run. She crossed the grass at a graceful, even pace, her head held high, her shoulders well back.

The cottage door was open and she didn't hesitate but entered at once. Rad was lying back in a chair while Shanie perched on his desk, prattling childishly. He was smiling in tolerant amusement, but the smile vanished as he saw Lesley and he got to his feet swiftly.

'Lesley, my darling girl, what is it?' he demanded urgently.

'I'm not your darling girl,' she said distractedly. Then she drew a deep breath and was able to continue in a frozen voice. 'All those times you told me that I possessed intelligence . . . My God, Rad, how you must have been laughing! Because I've really been very stupid, haven't I?'

'Lesley!' He grasped her shoulders, his fingers digging into her flesh. He looked back at the staring

Shanie. 'Get out of here, Shanie.'

'No, let her stay,' Lesley urged icily. 'It will amuse her. And take your hands off me, Rad.'

'This is a distinct change from the refrain of the last few days,' he drawled, but he let her go.

'I've a message for you,' Lesley went on with a breathless little laugh. 'From your newspaper. They really could do with that story on the Crosnier girl now, otherwise the whole thing is going to die on them.'

'My God! So that's it!' Rad stepped towards her again.

'You'd better sit down and write it, hadn't you?' she continued in the same quiet, deadly voice. 'It should make good reading for the public—and be accurate. After all, you know me ... intimately, don't you? There's just one thing, though ... do you journalists not have some sort of ethical code preventing you from becoming involved with the subjects of your stories? Like doctors and social workers? You should have, you know.'

'Lesley, will you shut up for a minute and listen to me?' Rad was furious.

'I don't think so, thank you.' She even managed a smile, an empty, over-bright smile, as she turned away from him.

Shanie's voice entered her mind. 'But Lesley, I can't understand what you're so angry about,' she protested guilelessly, blue eyes childishly wondering. 'If Rad is going to write about you, that's fair enough, surely? You can't complain when you yourself have talked of nothing but avenging yourself against him for the mess he made of your life when he exposed your father ... Why, even that first evening you were here, you told me what you were planning.'

Lesley didn't look at Shanie, although she heard her.

She had turned back and was watching the anger tautening Rad's face, seeing the furious darkening of his eyes.

'Is this true, Lesley?' he questioned her savagely.

Lesley stared at him. Part of her rebelled at the idea of his believing such a thing of her. Yet she couldn't bring herself to confess that those words about vengeance had been spoken without any such intention actually in her mind; Shanie had irritated her and she had amused herself by attempting to make the girl alarmed on Rad's behalf. Pride, all that she had left to her now, insisted that here was a gift to be turned to her own advantage.

'Yes, it's true,' she said simply and very coldly.

'You bitch! You——' She thought for a moment that he might strike her, but he didn't.

'Oh, why?' she enquired interestedly. 'As Shanie so shrewdly remarked, surely it's fair enough? You deceived me and I deceived you. Who's the winner?'

'May you be damned, Lesley,' said Rad in such an intense, dangerous voice that she managed a smile only with difficulty.

'And may you . . .' She stopped. 'It would take too long. Have fun holding me up to public ridicule, Rad. I admit my stupidity. I should have wondered why you were prepared to do so much for me. You were the clever one . . . But I still hope that . . . that you never know anything but hell, for the rest of your days, that you see things to give you endless nightmares, and never have another woman to listen to you, as I listened, and take the hell away . . . and never know the release of death. I hope there are lots of bullets and that none kills you!'

'A comprehensive and vicious curse, my dear,' he congratulated her sardonically.

'I could go on.'

'I'm sure you could, but those several fates will do quite adequately,' he told her. 'I should suffer, and that's what you want, isn't it? Now get out of here!'

'I'm going.'

She turned gracefully, glimpsing Shanie's face, curious, shocked and triumphant all at once.

Walking back to the main house was the hardest part of it, she found, but again she did not run. She felt chilled, chilled almost to death, the only sensation left to her being in her heart, and that she wanted to tear from her breast because otherwise the pain would go on and on for ever.

Yolande met her in the hall. Her sympathetically enquiring look drew an agonised moan from Lesley and the girl collapsed into motherly arms, shuddering uncontrollably, dry sobs of shock and grief racking her, but still not a tear falling from her dry, dazed and hurt-filled eyes.

CHAPTER TEN

'LESLEY, you must tell me what's happened,' Yolande insisted gently, having drawn her into the lounge and pushed her down into a chair, waving Michael away when he came to ask what was going on.

'I can't,' Lesley whispered. 'Oh God, oh God, oh God! Yolande, I've got to get away from here. Help me! My things are all packed upstairs . . . I was going to move in with Rad, and now . . . If you don't help me, I'll steal Mike's car, or better still, Rad's, or I'll hitch. I've got to get away! I can't stay!'

'Hush, Lesley,' Yolande urged. 'There's Rad in the hall now. I'm sure he'll . . . make everything right. If you were prepared to move in with him, there can't be anything irreparably wrong.'

'I can't see him!' Lesley said wildly, uncaring now that she had discarded self-control that Rad could probably hear her from the hall. 'I've got to get away, Yolande.'

'If that's really true, of course Mike and I will help you,' Yolande promised soothingly. 'But first let me go out and see if he can explain . . . I still don't know what's upset you so. Stay here.'

Lesley couldn't have moved had she wanted to. She remained where she was, staring at nothing.

From the hall came Rad's voice, harsher than she had ever heard it. 'You can tell her that she needn't go rushing away, Yolande. I'm the one who's leaving, now, just as soon as I've got a few things together. But first——'

Then the door between lounge and hall was deliberately shut, whether by Rad or Yolande, she didn't know, and she heard no more.

All that Yolande said later was, 'Rad is leaving, Lesley, so we'd like you to stay on, at least for a while. You're in no fit state to go anywhere at the moment, and I don't believe you've anywhere to go.'

Lesley's protest was merely a subdued murmur about feeling unable to impose on them, but she didn't labour it. Just now, she had neither the spirit nor the energy to care about anything, and the need to think clearly and make arrangements would have destroyed her.

All she could think about was her stupidity. She had known Rad didn't love her, but all that he had done for her had suggested that a measure of caring was added to his physical need of her. And all the time he had been using her, using or abusing her . . .

The trouble was that love, when it finally touched her, had been too deep, too complete, and she had eagerly given all of herself, humbly grateful for whatever he gave in return, even if it was less than she offered. Her only consolation now, and that to her pride alone, was his belief that she had somehow thought she was avenging his exposure of her father.

Later, she watched from a window as he drove away, and then went outside to a point from which she could see the red road between the citrus groves. The white car was speeding away, out of her life for ever, and soon all that remained to be seen was a cloud of red dust, slowly dispersing.

In the days that followed, Lesley discovered the meaning of intense, unrelieved anguish. For the Wards' sakes, she restrained her grief as best she could, storing it up during the days to be released in tears and agonised thought through the long, hot sleepless nights when her heart yearned for the tender caring she now knew herself to have imagined, and her body ached for Rad's with a terrible emptiness.

To a strangely subdued Shanie she could barely bring herself to be civil.

On New Year's Eve there was another party at the country club, a traditional ball, but Lesley chose to remain at the farm and no one pressed her to attend. When the others had departed, she found the key to the rondawel cottage hanging on its hook in the kitchen and, a little later, walked across the lawn and unlocked the door.

Johanna came to clean and air it every few days, but it still contained her and Rad, it seemed to Lesley's hyper-sensitive mind. Time-warped, she heard her voice and his in their various exchanges, and knew again his passionate possession. But the absence of his belongings gradually chilled her into aching reality. As he travelled so much, he had owned little to hamper him, so that now all his clothes were gone. All that remained were his books and records. Lesley lay down on the bed where she had known her entire sum of happiness; then a thought struck her and she got up again.

Frantically she searched the cottage from end to end, but the miniature of herself, her Christmas gift to him, was gone. A thousand questions in her mind, some so stupidly, stupidly hopeful . . . If it had gone away with him, it was undoubtedly by mistake. He had been angry and would have swept everything into his cases without noticing what went in.

When midnight came she was back in the main house. She turned on the radio to hear the chimes and Auld Lang Syne, and felt sickened by the sentiment and, later, by the gaiety of the medley playing. This wasn't a year she could meet with optimism, or even hope.

Shanie, she discovered the next day, had enjoyed the ball. Therefore Shanie was back to normal once more, and Lesley found her sweetness more of an irritant than ever before. It required several of her coldly impassive responses to the girl's overtures before Shanie stopped giving her childishly hurt looks and gave up trying to establish a friendship.

During the next few days, Lesley attempted several times to suggest to Michael and Yolande that it was time she left them and started looking for a job, but always they were at great pains to dissuade her.

'There's no hurry, surely,' Michael said at breakfast one morning, giving her a brief hug. 'None at all, and we want you to stay on. We like you.'

'Besides, Lesley,' Yolande picked up the subject again when Michael had gone out to join his labourers and Shanie too had departed, 'you're in no state to cope with a job. I know how shattered you are, although I still don't know what went wrong. Wait until you're feeling a little less devastated. You know me well enough to know that I'm not merely being the polite hostess. I want you to remain with us a while.'

And indeed, Lesley was able to know that their sympathy was genuine, that they didn't feel imposed on, that they were, in fact, considerably anxious that she should not depart yet.

'Thank you,' she said.

She knew too that they pitied her deep distress, but her pride did not rebel as it would once have done. She was no longer the girl who had always played a part; she didn't have the spirit to dissemble.

'And if it will help you, Shanie is going away to stay with a school friend,' Yolande resumed tentatively. 'I know she features somewhere in your unhappiness, Lesley. I don't know how or why, and I don't want to. Anyway, with Rad gone, she's a little bored and she'll only return to us for a few days before she has to go to Johannesburg for orientation week. So you see, more than ever, I'll be glad if you stay. I won't have my daughter, so you can take her place.'

So the days passed, in a haze of pain and regret, with Lesley flinching at any mention of Rad and resolutely avoiding even glancing at a newspaper, for the Wards took the one for which he wrote. She didn't want to know if he had done the article about her, nor what he might have written. If he had been too cruel, it might kill her.

She entertained the fear mingled with hope that Rad might have made her pregnant. How could she manage to bear and bring up a child on her own, unfitted as she was for any sort of job which would provide a sufficient income? Yet a child would be a memorial to her pitifully short time of happiness, and a part of the man whom she still loved, with a desperate, exalted love, despite what he had done to her.

On the day after Shanie's departure, Lesley discovered that there was no baby growing in her body. Rad had left her nothing of himself. She would have only memories, and remain cold and empty.

Her disappointment far outweighed her relief and she wept bitterly that day, beating her hands against the wall in her bedroom until her palms stung with pain and became bruised. Johanna, coming to dust and finding her in such a state, had been sufficiently perturbed to call Yolande and the older woman came to comfort her without questioning what might have brought about the terrible storm of grief. She looked at the distressed girl with growing concern, perhaps only now fully realising that the whole fragile structure that made up Lesley Ann had been cruelly rent.

She had loved utterly; therefore her betrayal destroyed her utterly even though she had never imagined for a moment that Rad loved her. She had merely thought him caring, and grateful for what she gave him, but even about that she had been wrong.

Yet there remained a core of strength in Lesley that forced her out of bed in the mornings to select her clothes with as much care as ever and put on her make-up, and which enabled her to say to Yolande one morning when the new year was two weeks old and they sat beside the pool with their coffee:

'Yolande, I mustn't go on like this. You and Mike have been wonderful, but it was Rad who was your friend, not me, and I know you're often uncomfortable and perplexed by this whole situation. I must leave you now and start supporting myself.'

'Lesley, you're as much our friend as Rad. If he . . .' Yolande stopped, looking down at her hands. 'I've been thinking about your problem and . . . Well, why not stay on here and get a local job, perhaps in Tzaneen? You could borrow my car for getting to work every day.'

Sensing that she genuinely wanted this, Lesley was prepared to consider it. 'I suppose it might be a good idea, considering my lack of qualifications. There'd be less competition than there would in one of the cities.'

'Then stay,' Yolande urged.

Lesley looked uncertain. 'I suppose it will be a long time before . . . before he comes here again? He's probably left to cover some war by now, don't you think?'

'I expect so,' Yolande said vaguely. She looked at Lesley and sighed. 'Oh, my dear, I wish I could say more. I wish I could help you more.'

'You're too generous already,' Lesley protested. She tried a smile, but it didn't work.

Yolande shook her head. 'Don't try so hard, Lesley. You need time. All the same, I've noticed . . . Well, perhaps if you didn't keep going over to the rondawel cottage?'

'I can't keep away from it.' Lesley lifted her head proudly, but her cheeks were flushed. 'We were lovers, you know.'

'I guessed,' Yolande said calmly. 'Are you pregnant?'

'No. That's why . . . I cried like that, the morning when Johanna called you,' Lesley confessed with difficulty. Her eyes went dark with agony. 'You see, I wanted to be. It was so personal that I hoped . . . Oh, God, Yolande! When will it end? I can't bear it if it goes on for ever. Will I always hurt like this?'

She was sobbing terribly, sorrowfully, and Yolande was out of her chair and beside her in an instant, comforting her as her own mother would never have done, showing the compassion that no other woman save her grandmother had ever shown to Lesley.

But even when she was calm once more and apologising for her outburst, the older woman's hazel eyes remained disturbed.

'You can't help it,' she cut short the girl's apologies. 'Oh, my poor darling, whoever doesn't believe that hearts can break should meet you. It's what they call . . . deathless passion, isn't it?'

And Lesley could only nod.

She swam after lunch that day, then changed into jeans and a fuchsia top and went down to the kitchen to get the key to the cottage, relieved at not encountering Yolande, for she felt guiltily ashamed of her weakness.

This would be the last time, she promised herself as she let herself into the cottage. She had promised the same thing yesterday.

She wandered aimlessly through the rooms, seeking nothing in particular because there was nothing to seek. Yet the place held her in thrall because for her it was time-locked, this scene of her entry into womanhood.

Eventually, finding herself in the bedroom, she lay down on the bed and closed her eyes. What had she hoped to achieve by coming here again? She was a fool, and always had been, and now she must accept pain as her lot and take it from there.

But a few slow tears rolled from beneath her eyelids. Where was he now? Her lover, who had never really been a lover because there was no commitment in his heart. She had never asked for or expected love, and she had known he must go away when his leave was over without any suggestion of there being a permanent future for them. These things were cause merely for regret; her intense, unending pain stemmed from the knowledge of his betrayal of her. That last morning when their lovemaking had had that rarefied quality, that desperation—she should have known then, she realised.

Eventually sheer exhaustion, the result of sleepless nights, caught up with her. This morning's storm of weeping had meant overload and her physical resources could no longer cope with the emotional demands made on them.

The tears stopped and Lesley slept.

Rad Sinclair entered the rondawel cottage silently, more deeply concerned that he had revealed while listening to Yolande's report.

The door leading to the bedroom stood open and through it he could see the bed and the dark-haired girl lying on it. He felt as if he had entered a time-slip—only on the last occasion he had seen her lying there, he had been beside her.

He paused at the door, his imagination stirred by her stillness. She looked so cold, like a figure carved from marble, or a corpse, beautiful but waxen. He heard again her voice as it had sounded when, out of her pain, she had damned him, with a curse that revealed all too clearly the depth of her understanding of his needs—a curse which had haunted him vividly for more than two weeks.

'. . . and never know the release of death.' He remembered her tone too well.

But then the corners of his mouth tilted. That would never be Lesley Ann's way. She was bright and brave, and whatever happened to her, her heartbreakingly beautiful smile would eventually flash out again to deceive the world.

The even rise and fall of her breasts was reassuring as he came to stand beside the bed. He stifled an exclamation as he saw that she had been crying. The beautiful make-up which was so vital a prop to her act was as skilfully done as ever, but the traitorous tracks of her tears revealed the bruised tiredness beneath her eyes. He studied her intently, noting too the hollows beneath her classically high cheekbones and the shadowy suggestion of fragility at her temples.

A moment of self-loathing tautened his features, for he knew how her proud, vulnerable nature would hate his seeing her like this.

Yet he remained where he was, standing beside the bed and looking down at her, watching her sleep as he had watched her before when he lay beside her, and never finding a flaw in all that strong-delicate beauty.

Eventually, however, he stirred impatiently. He had been travelling for what seemed like a lifetime and his need for one of those slow, measured looks from shadowy green eyes was irresistible.

He sat down carefully on the edge of the bed and laid one hand flat against the side of her neck. Beneath his palm was smoothness and warmth and a flickering pulse, while against the back of his hand her curls were a silken caress.

'Lesley.'

She was instantly awake, her eyes fluttering open. She stared up at him, first with incredulity and pain, and then with fear.

'Rad.'

'It's a crime to wake you, I know.' Briefly his fingertips caressed the line of her jaw and were removed.

Lesley stared at him warily, noting the signs of fatigue about his darkly grey eyes and the vertical lines at either side of his mouth. She gulped, fighting panic. She had never been in such a desperate situation before, with no idea how to react or what to say. It seemed the ultimate cruelty for him to take her unawares like this, with no defensive act prepared.

'What are you doing here?' she asked eventually in a low, strained voice. 'I imagined you'd be overseas by this time.'

'I've been overseas and come back,' Rad told her.

'What for?' she tried to sound cool.

'To keep a promise.' He shrugged casually enough, but she was aware of the tension in his face and in his body. 'Or to make reparation.'

'I don't believe it,' she said flatly.

He sighed and she resisted a wild temptation to reach out and draw him to her and drain the weariness from him with her lips and hands.

'I've been scouring Europe in search of your father,' he told her expressionlessly. 'I kept arriving at some place he and your mother had been in, only to find that they'd moved on a few hours earlier. They're living nomadically, never stopping anywhere for long. Eventually, however, the attractions of sophisticated society caused them to linger in Kitzbühel a little too long, and that's where I found them. Lesley, I once promised you that you would finish your university course, and you will, if that's what you want. Since you would never have allowed me to pay your fees, I had to find your father and get him to do his duty by you. I persuaded him, by means of a few unpleasant threats and many harsh words, to part with an amount approximate to that which you'll require in order to complete your course. I insisted on cash . . . there are exchange control regulations to be sorted out, of course, but you can open a bank account and I'll transfer the same amount to it. Your father owes a lot of money to a great many people, but he also owes you something, so you can accept it as your right.'

Lesley looked at him indifferently. 'Thank you. I won't say that it was the least you could do because . . . I didn't expect it of you. I didn't expect anything.'

'That's your whole trouble!' His control snapped. 'You didn't expect, you didn't believe, you didn't have faith!'

'How could I have?' she challenged simply. Then, lightly and with a brittle smile, 'How fitting that you should be the one to finally track down my father, when you were the one to uncover his activities in the first place. Another scoop for your paper, with your name above the report!'

'Wrong,' Rad said tautly. 'Naturally I let my colleagues know where I'd finally found Gerard Crosnier and they can cover it as they think fit. But my search for him was a personal and private matter, although naturally my status as a pressman proved useful, and I haven't written a word about it. It wasn't as a journalist that I interviewed your father.'

'You preferred to write about the daughter.' A world of sadness lay in her voice. Her control gave way suddenly. 'How could you do it, Rad? How could you do that to me?'

His hands slid beneath her and he pulled her up into his arms, holding her very tightly. 'I didn't do that to you, Lesley,' he said furiously. 'I never wrote a word about you, for pity's sake. I never even considered doing so for one moment. When I called my paper in response to the message they'd left with you on Boxing Day, they raised the idea and I refused, immediately and finally. They were reluctant to accept that and suggested that I think it over and they'd call back in a couple of days for my decision. It's a way of theirs, when I've been reluctant to undertake something, to pretend to take it for granted that I'll eventually agree, which is why the second message came across as it did. I've now resigned from that paper, partly because of their presumption in expecting me to descend to such a low level of journalism, and partly because I've been offered a far better post on a London publication . . . But dear God, Lesley, how could you think I'd do that to you? You knew my reputation as a journalist, yet you believed I'd sink to the level of a gossip columnist. Above all, you knew what you'd been to me . . . After what we'd shared, how could you believe such a thing of me? How could you?' His voice was hoarse and intense, full of anger and—pain, she thought as she stirred protestingly at the pressure he was exerting. He held her so tightly and now she felt him shudder convulsively. A moment later he let her drop back against the pillows. 'Oh, hell! I'm hurting you . . . I'm sorry. But, Lesley, couldn't you have trusted me?'

She shook her head as tears of bitter regret spilled from her agonised eyes. 'How could I trust in . . . happiness when it was so new to me, when I'd had such a short time of it? I was defensive, afraid of its ending . . . expecting it to end.'

Rad went very still. 'I should have known,' he said quietly. 'I ought to have made sure you had complete faith in . . . in what we had. I failed you, Lesley.'

'It doesn't matter,' she said wearily. 'Rad, I don't suppose anything matters now that it's over, but I'd like you to know that although what Shanie said . . . although I did talk to her of revenge, I never actually felt any resentment against you for what you'd brought about by exposing my father's activities. She . . . she would go on and on about you, and it amused me to alarm her. I never deceived you.'

'I realised that within minutes of your walking out of this cottage, darling,' Rad said gently.

'You . . .?' Colour stained her cheeks.

'I know you rather well, my dear,' he went on. 'I guessed that such talk had probably been part of your act with Shanie . . . I gave that kid hell when I realised what she'd attempted to do. I decided it would help you to continue believing I thought you'd been deceiving me . . . help your pride. Anyway, I couldn't bring myself to see you again before I left because I was still so angered by your lack of trust. I could only beg Mike and Yolande to keep you here at all costs, and then go and do what I knew I must.'

Lesley expelled a shuddering sigh and tried to smile through her tears. 'So now it's all over. I'll be going back to Varsity and you'll be leaving South Africa——'

'In about two weeks' time, but——'

Despair found voice. 'Oh God, Rad, what will I do without you? Why do I have to love you so much? How will I survive?'

In a moment he was lying beside her, cradling her in his arms and kissing the tears from her cheeks before burying his face in her hair.

'You don't have to do without me,' he said urgently. 'Because I can't do without you, my darling . . . my dearest love. I need you, all of my life!'

'I don't believe you.' Her voice cracked.

'You've got to,' Rad insisted on a note of desperation, his hands possessive as they caressed her body fiercely. 'I'll never forgive myself for making you suffer, as I know you have, Lesley. I never even told you I loved you. I could have phoned you from Europe, but I thought you'd refuse to speak to me and that it was better to wait until I returned . . . I know how badly you've been hurting and I'm not worth such suffering, or such love . . . My darling, I love you endlessly. I think I've always loved you, although I only began to suspect it that morning when I found you hiding under a sheet because you didn't want me to see you without your make-up. I love everything about you; your courage and your cleverness, the act you put on, your thousand smiles . . . I love your beauty and the sweet heaven of your body, and I love your generosity and your understanding. You're such a pure . . . complete woman. You gave me everything.'

Drawing back and seeing the truth blazing from his eyes, and seeing him clearly as she had not done before, Lesley sighed, at last laying down the load of her hopelessness and finding herself in possession of such a treasure as she had never thought to hold, Rad's love.

'If you're able to find and love all those things in me, my darling, it's only because you made me a complete woman,' she told him, her voice a silvery thread of sound as she wound her slim arms about his neck.

Their long kisses were a commitment; there was a flow of love between them, uniting them.

Rad said, 'Lesley, I want——' He stopped. 'No, I promised myself that I wouldn't demand. I'll ask . . . request. Will you marry me? Here, at Duiwelskloof, as soon as possible? And then in a couple of weeks' time we'll go to London where you can continue your studies if you like. Can you do that for me, darling? Initially we may have to be apart for short periods, but I'll be facing less dangerous situations now, and one day when we have a child I'll be with you and there'll be no more partings.'

'I'll marry you, Rad.' Lesley's eyes were luminous and her smile a thing of pure beauty as she slid her fingers between the buttons of his cream shirt.

'And go to London with me?'

'And go wherever you ask me to.'

'Are you sure?' Strangely, he was uncertain.

'Don't look at me like that,' she protested on a little gasp. 'Rad, you must now how much I love you!'

'I do know,' he groaned, turning her on to her back and lowering his body to hers, his hands parting her clothes. Their lips clung and desire for the ultimate expression of their love surged through them. 'I've been in hell these last two weeks, wanting you—the sight of you, the sound of you . . . I'd look at your miniature portrait and ache for the real thing.'

Lesley spoke jerkily as Rad's lips caressed her smooth, firm breasts. 'Rad, if—you loved me, why did you bother looking for my father and securing the chance for me to return to Varsity?'

He lifted his head to look at her and what she saw in his face made her catch her breath.

'I wanted you to have a choice,' he said simply.

Lesley's eyes were lit with wonder, worshipping. 'You . . . that much?' she whispered.

'That much, my darling,' Rad confirmed quietly.

Then not a doubt remained in her. Her fingers caressed his face. 'I'll be everything to you, Rad,' she promised with lilting joy, and with pride. 'I'll be everything you need me to be, my darling.'

'I've never doubted it,' he retorted tenderly. 'Your

greatest gift is your ability to love.'

'And I love you.' She drew his head down to her breasts again, her love and gratitude making her trem-ble. 'Oh, Rad, my darling, how . . . equally we love, because you are also everything to me, my life and my world . . .'

A long time later, Lesley's mouth curved beautifully and rapture still shone in her eyes as she looked up into Rad's face.

'I must look a wreck!'

He smiled with infinite tenderness, utterly at peace in the aftermath of passion.

'You look beautiful to me . . . my future wife.' His lips touched the smudges about her eyes. 'What's a little mascara between lovers?'

'The best pair of lovers in the world,' Lesley said complacently.

They both laughed, and presently set about proving it again.

Mills & Boon Reader Film Service

special attention resulting in a short delay. Obviously the postal time must be added and we cannot eliminate the possibility of an occasional delay here but your film should take no longer than 7 days door-to-door.

What you get

Superprints giving 30% more picture area than the old style standard enprint. Print sizes as follows:

Print Size	from 35mm	from 110	from 126
Superprints	4″ × 5¾″	4″ × 5⅛″	4″ × 4″

All sizes approximate.
All prints are borderless, have round corners and a sheen surface.

Prices

No developing charge, you only pay for each successful print:
Superprints 22p each.
This includes VAT at the current rate and applies to 100 ASA film only. Prices apply to UK only. There is no minimum charge.
We handle colour negative film for prints only and Superprints can only be made from 35mm, 126 and 110 film which is for C41 process.

If you have any queries 'phone 0734 597332 or write to: Customer Service, Mills & Boon Reader Film Service, P.O. Box 180, Reading RG1 3PF.